PRAISE FOR

Here are some of the over 100,000 five star reviews left for the Dead Cold Mystery series.

"Rex Stout and Michael Connelly have spawned a protege."

AMAZON REVIEW

"So begins one damned fine read."

AMAZON REVIEW

"Mystery that's more brain than brawn."

AMAZON REVIEW

"I read so many of this genre...and ever so often I strike gold!"

AMAZON REVIEW

"This book is filled with action, intrigue, espionage, and everything else lovers of a good thriller want."

AMAZON REVIEW

FALLEN ANGELS

A DEAD COLD MYSTERY

BLAKE BANNER

RIGHTHOUSE

ISBN-13: 978-1-63696-026-5

ISBN-10: 1-63696-026-X

Cover design by: Damonza

Printed in the United States of America

www.righthouse.com

www.instagram.com/righthousebooks

www.facebook.com/righthousebooks

twitter.com/righthousebooks

DEAD COLD MYSTERY SERIES

ONE

It was dark.

I sat a moment in my car, with the windows down, thinking about Billy Crystal in *Throw Momma from the Train*. The night was hot, the night was muggy, the night was oppressive and sticky. The night was sultry.

I was parked on Bolton Avenue, near the corner with Lacombe, outside a large, blue-gray clapboard house that stood in its own plot of land with a small garden in the front yard. Its porch lights were on, and Dehan was standing in the middle of the road with her hands in her pockets, looking back at me, frowning slightly among a smile. She was wearing a T-shirt and a bun, low on her neck. She also looked more than a little sultry.

As well as Dehan, there were three patrol cars making red lights dart here and there against the walls of the houses, there was an ambulance from the ME's department, and Frank the ME's car. Then there was the crime scene team's van and Sam Epstein's Jeep.

Dehan said, "You coming, or do you want to video conference?"

"I was thinking," I said, and climbed out of my ancient

Jaguar. I slammed the door and joined her, and we crossed the road together. She sighed and shook her head.

"So soon? We just got here and already you're thinking? How am I supposed to compete with that?"

"Compete? Why would you want to compete with me?"

Sergeant O'Brien was at the gate talking to a rookie. He greeted us and raised the tape for us to pass under, then pointed toward the steps up to the porch.

"'Tective Epstein's inside. Vic's in the dining room at the back." He shifted his pale eyes to Dehan and gave his big Irish head a twitch. "It ain't nice."

She shook her head. "Such a letdown. Last murder I was at rocked."

He leaned back and wheezed a laugh as we walked away. "She's a one!" I heard him say. "I tell you, she's a one!"

We climbed the steps and moved across the threshold into a brightly lit living room with a staircase rising to the second floor on the left, a fireplace, comfortable armchairs and a sofa, bookcases with real, well-used books, and lamps on lamp tables. A couple of Joe's boys were going around on their hands and knees, dressed like spacemen, dusting and spraying and picking minute things off the carpets. One of them was taking photographs.

But the real action was through the arch, in the dining area. Dehan stopped dead in her tracks and whispered, "What the hell . . ."

Epstein was standing with his hands on his hips and an expression on his face like he'd just found the Bolognese sauce he'd made six months ago and forgotten about. On the floor I could see Frank's hunched back, and just beyond it a man. You couldn't say he was lying on his face, because he had no face left to lie on, but he was lying on his belly, and the floor and the carpet where his head should have been were awash with blood and gore.

A couple of paces away from him was the dining table, which had apparently been moved from its habitual position, and on it was a complicated arrangement with a box and a drip-stand.

There was also a cat box, and by the sound it was making, there was a cat inside it.

I gently propelled Dehan forward, and we both looked in the direction the shot had come from. There was nothing there but a large painter's easel with a shotgun clamped to it by means of a couple of vices. Detective Epstein turned to look at us. He didn't say "good morning," even though it was three o'clock in the a.m. Instead he said, "Boy, am I glad to see you two!"

Dehan glanced at me. Her face said she was bewildered. "I don't think anybody has ever said that to me before. And I know for damn sure nobody has ever said it about . . ." She indicated us both with her finger, back and forth, and Epstein frowned at her, like she was speaking French to him.

I said, "I'm guessing this case relates back to a cold case, that's why we have been from our beds untimely ripped."

Frank turned and looked up at me from the mangled corpse. "Seriously? *Macbeth?* At three a.m.?" To Dehan he said, "How do you live with him?"

Epstein winced. "What?"

Dehan pointed at what was left of the body and said, "Cold case connected?"

He nodded, said, "Yeah," then frowned at me and said, "Who's Macbeth?"

"A Scottish regicide. You wouldn't know him. Tell me about the case."

"Chief says to hand it over to you guys. I tell you, I'm glad to. It's been get'n on my nerves." He clenched his fists to show just how much it had been getting on his nerves. "You done, Doc? I want to show John and Carmen here just what went down."

Frank snorted and said, "Good luck. Be very careful where you tread. I want as much of that brain matter and blood as I can get back at the lab. Make it snappy and let Joe's boys in."

The gurney rattled in. They put the decapitated corpse in the body bag and lifted it onto the trolley, then wheeled it out to the ambulance. Frank went with it, and as it passed through the door,

Epstein beckoned us into the dining area. We stepped in, avoiding the gore, and looked around. There was a threadbare, Persian-style rug where you could see the impressions made by the four table legs over many years. But the table had been moved over to the left, in front of where the corpse had been lying.

Epstein said, "See? Whoever it is does these things, he's come in and he's tied this poor bastard to a chair, right there . . ."

He pointed to a chair that was lying on its side, about six feet from the table, and a couple of feet in front of the easel with the shotgun.

"Wait, stop." It was Dehan with one hand raised. "Let me see if I get this. Who is this guy, the victim?"

"Reginald Jensen, sixty-six, retired bank manager."

"So the intruder ties Reggie to that bentwood chair, places this table in front of him, and the easel behind him . . ."

"That's what I said. But here's the crazy thing. Reggie could have sat there all night and nothin' would have happened. When the postman came, or whatever, he could have shouted and hollered and *somebody* would have heard him. The only reason the damned gun went off was because he moved forward. He had a string in his hand. He pulls the string, the knots come undone, and he can move. But if he moves, he has a string around his neck, on a pulley . . . see? So whichever way he goes, forward, backward, sideways, it pulls the trigger and blows his head off. But if he waited, he'd be okay."

I was looking at the table, thinking that if the killer put him looking at the table it was because there was something on the table that he wanted him to look at and think about, possibly to make him move. Dehan was frowning, staring at the chair on the floor. "So . . . ?"

Epstein was nodding big nods, with his mouth sagging open slightly and releasing small, single laughs. "Right?" he said, and then again, "Right? Well get this. Jensen loves cats, he's got like a hundred books on cats, but the cat he is most crazy about is Siddhartha here." He pointed at the cat basket on the table where a tabby and white cat was lying, gazing at us with detached interest.

"How do you know he's called Siddhartha?"

"It's on his bowl in the kitchen. Anyhow, the son of a bitch killer knows this. So he ties Jensen to the chair, with the contraption behind him tied to his neck, and he gets Siddhartha and he puts him in that box . . ." He pointed to the carton on the table. "But that ain't no ordinary box. It's like that guy who wanted to prove things are only real when you see them . . ." He snapped his fingers a few times.

I said, "Schrödinger."

"Yeah." He leered at Dehan. "I knew it, if anyone is going to know the name, it'll be Stone, right? So it's like Schrödinger's cat. The box is set up with a timer and a small detonator that, after fifteen minutes, is going to release something into the air inside the box. Joe's already bagged it for the lab. My guess is it's going to be some very painful nerve gas . . ."

I interrupted, pointing at the box, which had a long, blood-soaked string attached. "That string . . ."

He gave a few more of his exaggerated nods while he interrupted me back. "Exactly, it was a few inches from his right hand. If he reached for it and pulled it, it killed the timer, but it also triggered the shotgun. I think that's what you'd call diabolical, right? Son of a bitch. But the weirdest thing, thing that makes your blood go cold, was the music. Pen drive stuck in the sound system playing classical music."

I suppressed a sigh and raised an eyebrow. "Classical?"

He grinned and pointed at me. "I knew you'd do that. I said, Stone ain't gonna be satisfied with 'classical music.' So I asked Frank what it was. He said it was Italian, sacred, ren . . ."

"Renaissance."

"That's it. That's what he said."

I nodded. "So he's giving Jensen a choice: save your cat and die, or let your cat die in pain, and save yourself."

Epstein held up both hands like I'd pointed a gun at him. "A guy like you or me, no contest, right?" He laughed. "But for a guy like Jensen." He shrugged, tilting his head on one side. "Guys like him, lonely, sensitive . . . you know what I'm sayin'?"

Dehan muttered, "Son of a bitch," and then asked, "So what's this got to do with us?"

I interrupted before he could answer. "You said earlier, 'Whoever it is does these things . . .' So he, or she, has done this before, it's gone cold, now you think it's gone hot again and you want us to take it."

He winced and shrugged at the same time. "The chief. Me? I'd take it, see it through, know what I mean? But the chief figures you guys got a feel for cold cases . . ."

Dehan looked at me and pulled down the corners of her mouth. "The Schrödinger's Cat Killer?"

I smiled. "No."

She arched both eyebrows high. "The You're-Only-Dead-If-They-Find-You Killer?"

I shook my head. "Actually, Schrödinger was trying to prove the opposite. His thought experiment was intended to show how stupid that view was, but as it turned out that view was right, and he and Einstein were wrong."

Epstein was staring at me with his mouth slightly open. He turned to Dehan. "See? Nobody likes him, but you have to admit he's smart."

Dehan squinted at him and then at me.

"Nothing is real unless we look at it? Somebody put Pink Floyd on the record player, I'll get the acid. Where's the maharishi when you need him? It's a good job there are nearly eight billion of us, or the whole damn planet would disappear!"

"Which was kind of Schrödinger's point. But I don't think that's what this killer was about. This killer is about salvation. Are you connecting this case with the Georgina Cheng case a year ago?"

He spread his hands at Dehan. "See, this is why nobody likes him."

"It was on TV, but I remember you and Hank talked about it. She was a vivisectionist, and she was vocal about how we needed to perform vivisections for medical reasons."

"That's the one."

Dehan was nodding. "She was fed curare and tortured while she was conscious. Frank said she died of shock."

I added, "There was a pen drive in the sound system playing sacred music, but as I recall, that was English Tudor music, John Tallis, I think, 'Kyrie.'"

Dehan grunted. "Hell, some religious nut trying to get people to repent."

I asked Epstein, "How many victims are you attributing to this killer?"

"With this one, a total of six. One a year for the past six years."

Joe approached us. "Okay, guys, gonna have to ask you to move somewhere else. Let's go!"

We moved out to the living room. Epstein stood in the open doorway, and Dehan sat on the third step leading to the upper floor. Epstein was talking, but he had one foot out the door.

"At first it didn't look like a serial killer. They were just kind of random. It was the third one that got us thinking, you know, there is some kind of a link between these cases. I'll leave the file on your desk with all the details."

"Just give me an outline of the other four before you run off, will you?" I gave him a smile that wasn't much of a smile, and he sighed.

"First victim, September 2015. Ana Orcera, single mother. She'd just taken her kid to school. On the way back she'd been to her local church. Her boyfriend was out. He was some kind of bum, from Sudan or something. He was a suspect for a while. So when she got home the killer was waiting for her. Broke her arms and legs, stabbed her in the gut, and left her to bleed to death, listening to classical, sacred music.

"Second victim, February 2016, Mathew Cavendish, a financier and a philanthropist. Tied to his dining table, with the gas turned on, but this time the music was weird Japanese music, some kind of flute, jerky kind of stuff."

"Zen."

"Yeah, that's it. Weird, jerky."

I grunted, and he went on. "Third victim, November 2017, Saul Arender, criminal attorney, defended some very bad people and got a lot of them off on technicalities. He was hanged. It was elaborate, a bit like this case, the killer used ropes and pulleys in such a way that the victim's own attempts to escape caused him to be choked and decapitated. He used a piano wire as a noose. That was nasty. That time it was Tibetan bells.

"Fourth victim, June 2018, Judge Jeremiah Jones, known as Three Jay, the hanging judge. He handed out some pretty severe sentences along with a few lectures and sermons—he was an evangelist—but I gotta say I never thought he went too far. He was impaled with a decorative, ceremonial sword he had in his office. He was bound on the floor, and the sword was suspended from a rope over his chest. It was tough because he could see the rope being burned by a candle, and he couldn't move. With him it was, uh"—he snapped his fingers—"Gregorian chants."

Dehan asked him, "What about suspects?"

He winced and shook his head. "We never really got a solid lead on anybody. We thought about . . . uh . . ." He looked up at the ceiling. "Abdo Deng? Something like that. It's in the file. Ana Orcera's partner. But he didn't fit the profile at all. Then we had Reverend Morton Wells on our suspect list, but we couldn't really tie him to anything. There was no forensic evidence, and there were no damned witnesses."

"What made the reverend a suspect?"

"He was a priest, I forget what kind, I'm not big on religion. Must have been some kind of Protestant because he worked as a teacher in a Protestant school, but he was kicked out—of the school and the church—over allegations of child abuse. The allegations were never proven, but the shit stuck, and they preferred to get shot of him. He later opened his own ministry down on Leland Avenue and Soundview. Ironic, his big thing is the sanctity of the family, the power of forgiveness, and the 'divine grace in rebirth.' Thing is, Ana Orcera, the first victim, was in his congregation for a while, then switched to the Catholic church one block away on Thieriot. A few days before she was killed, he was seen visiting her. It ain't a lot to go on, but it was about all we had. The day she was killed she dropped the kid at the school on Thieriot, crossed Randall to the church a hundred yards away, spoke to the padre there, then went home. Now, her shortest route home is right past Morton Wells' mission."

I grunted. "Any other connections to her or any of the other victims?"

He sighed, pulled a pack of Lucky Strikes from his pocket, offered us a cigarette, and asked if we minded. I shook my head, and he lit up. Blowing smoke into the predawn darkness, he looked away down the road.

"Nah . . . I mean, they was tenuous links. Know what I mean? But they made you feel there was more you weren't seein'. He was at Drew University with Mathew Cavendish, the second victim. They were both part of the debating club. Cavendish was a committed atheist *and* a philanthropist. Apparently they had a few debates, in and out of the club." He flicked ash. "Saul Arender was known to him, and he mentioned him in a few sermons, along the lines that as a criminal attorney and a Jew, he was a servant of Satan. He also preached against Georgina Cheng, the fifth victim."

Dehan said, "That leaves the judge and Jensen."

He shook his head. "No links that we ever found with the judge." He shrugged. "This case? What can I say? Aside from the fact that Morton's church is . . ." He stuck his arm out rigid, pointing at the house. "Exactly there, one hundred and fifty yards away, two houses away—aside from that, my gut tells me the connections are there."

He took another drag, dropped the butt on the ground, and,

with his hands shoved in his pockets, ground it into the concrete. Then he smiled at us.

"You guys have fun with the case. Maybe you're the ones to crack it. See you around."

With that he turned and slouched his way out of the gate toward his Jeep.

TWO

WE DID THE ROUNDS OF THE HOUSE, INCLUDING THE rooms upstairs, and found very little other than evidence that this was a man who lived alone and his only real companion was his cat, Siddhartha. But you didn't get a feeling of real loneliness from his home. Real loneliness carries with it despair, and despair expresses itself most often as either excessive order or chaos. There was neither in Jensen's house. It was clean, tidy, and well ordered, but not obsessively so.

In his bedroom, Dehan picked up a couple of books from his bedside table. "Looks like he was interested in Buddhism."

I had also noticed the books, and the small statue in the living room. I nodded, inspecting the inside of his wardrobe and his few clothes.

"Theravada."

"Isn't that a planet in *Star Trek*?"

I smiled but didn't let her see it. "You know it's not. It's the oldest form of Buddhism, practiced mainly in Sri Lanka, I believe."

"Is it important?"

I got to my feet from where I had crouched to inspect a drawer. "I don't know. Maybe. Some people say that Theravada, amongst the different styles of Buddhism, is most concerned with karma, or as they call it, *kamma*."

She thrust her hands in her pockets and frowned. "Retribution?"

"Not exactly." I shook my head. "There is no retribution in Buddhism. It's much more complex than that. It's more to do with cause and effect, but state of mind and intention are central to the doctrine. A very simplistic example would be . . ." I searched my mind. "If you are habitually absentminded and fail to be present in the moment, for example, and you get up from your chair and carry your glass to the kitchen, knock your hand on the corner of the table, and the glass falls and breaks. That is not retribution, it is simply a consequence of your mental attitude."

"Okay, and when you sweep it up, you continue to be careless and leave shards on the floor. Next morning when you come down barefoot you cut yourself, so the consequences can project into the future."

"Add to that the Buddhist ideas of reincarnation and that everything is, so to speak, mind, and you wind up with a surprisingly complex theory."

She grunted and narrowed her eyes, which meant she was thinking deeply. "So we have a victim who believes in karma, and a killer who seems to want to bring retribution . . ."

"Quite a coincidence, I agree."

She sat on the corner of the bed with her hands between her knees. "And the cat," she said. "They believe people can be reincarnated as animals, right?"

"Something like that."

"So it might have been really important for him to save the cat because it was his mother or something?"

I didn't really buy it, and I screwed up my face to show it. "I'm no expert, but I don't think it's quite like that. Maybe he just loved his cat and he was prepared to make that sacrifice to save it."

She shrugged. "Maybe. We are assuming a lot from a couple of books and a small statue. We don't even know for sure that he *was* a Buddhist, or whether that was relevant."

I agreed and nodded. "Anything else you need to see here?" She shook her head, then said, "Yeah, I want to see how this killer got in. The windows are all closed and intact. The back door is locked from the inside, which only leaves the front door. I want to know if he broke in, or if Jensen let him in."

"Yup, let's go have a look."

We found Joe, the head of the crime scene team, dusting the lock and taking photographs of it, inside and out.

"Did he break in, or was he let in?"

He laughed. "I can't tell you that, John. But I can tell you that this lock was not forced. Did he have a replica key? Was the door open when he arrived? I don't know. But I can tell you that he did not pick this lock."

We thanked him and walked down to where my old burgundy Jag was waiting for us. Dehan opened the passenger door, but I rested my ass on the hood and sat looking at the house. A breath of cool predawn air touched my face and made me shudder. Dehan's voice came from over my shoulder.

"What? First you didn't want to get out of the car, now you don't want to get in. You turning temperamental on me, big guy?"

I smiled over my shoulder at her, and she came and rested her ass next to mine. "I am just trying to visualize what happened." I shook my head. "If Reverend Morton Wells killed everyone in New York who had a different religion from his own, there would be a ten-year waiting list to get murdered by him."

She gave me a quick once-over with her eyes. "That is a very dark notion, Stone."

"My point is that what this killer does . . ." I sighed. "That's a lot of attention to pay somebody. There must be thousands of people in New York who are interested in Buddhism, and at least half of those probably have a cat."

"Why?"

"I don't know, it just seems to work that way. Buddhists have cats. It's a thing. The point is, what made *this particular* Buddhist with a cat different to all the rest, and worth killing in such a cruel way?"

She grunted. "Cruel and . . ."

She screwed up her face, and I said, "Cruel, and well-informed, and . . ."

I shook my head, and she said, "*Accurate!*"

"Yes," I said, and nodded. "Accurate. He had him down to a T. Even the little touch of Schrödinger. Everything is mind, which was pretty much what Schrödinger was trying to disprove with his thought experiment."

We were quiet for a moment. Then she put her hand on my shoulder. "Most serial killers are stupid, Stone. But I have a bad feeling we have a smart one here."

"Is he, or she, a serial killer?"

"Whoa! Seriously?"

"I'm not sure he's killing without motive. There's a lot about his actions that suggests motive. Also, if you look at each case, assuming they were all committed by the same person, the victims are not selected by type, by sex, by profession—in fact there seems to be no common feature to the victims at all, but in each case he kills them in such a way as to give them time to think about their death, and he plays sacred music designed to make them reflect on it. That definitely suggests a motive to me. But more than that, it suggests a fairly deep knowledge of each victim's personality." I hesitated, not wanting to go too far. "Or at least of the victims and their *moral* life."

She was silent, thinking about it. Then she said, "That's pretty far-fetched."

I nodded. "I agree, but it's no less true for that."

"So, what? We are looking for some kind of spiritual vigilante?"

"Or a fallen angel."

By the time we got to the 43rd it was almost six a.m. As

promised, the file was on my desk, with a copy for Dehan. I went to get a couple of buckets of coffee-like black liquid, and we sat and started going through the files.

There were profiles on the victims, crime scene photos which were mostly pretty harrowing, forensic reports, and details of interviews with Reverend Morton Wells and Abdo Deng, Ana Orcera's boyfriend. Outside the window there was a strip of luminous blue-gray skirting a black sky, and here and there, dappled orange streetlamps peppered the black glass through restless leaves. My head ached and my eyes wanted to sleep. I said aloud, "Abdo Deng, why are we discarding him as a suspect?"

She did something between a growl and a sigh, which was distracting, and said, "Our friend Epstein hasn't done a great job of putting this all together. He's a street cop, not a collator of evidence. Abdo Deng first shows up in Ana Orcera's profile. He was a short-term boyfriend-cum-lover of hers shortly before she died. Had a reputation for violence. Seems like they called him in mainly on the strength of that, just to talk to him."

I found the place and nodded as I read. "Uh-huh, interviewed him and didn't like him much, so they did a background check. Seems he was suspected of violent crimes in the Sudan . . ."

"Including rape and the murder of several young girls and women. Entered this country as a refugee, had ties with militant Islamic groups, but seems not to be active. Now works as a taxi driver."

"Interesting," I said. "A taxi can form a matrix of connections which, unless you know about the cab, seems utterly random. I wonder how he comes across in the interviews."

She was staring at the file in front of her. "I'm just reading through them now. So far he comes across as a miserable, surly bastard." She glanced at me over the page. "You're thinking that maybe he's really chatty in the cab and gets to know people that way?"

I gave a small shrug. "Maybe he connects with them, gets their addresses, is able to follow them . . . Maybe he's a lot more sociable when he's not being interrogated by cops."

"Yeah, maybe. That seems to be about it. A few people were looked at, but all had alibis for one killing or another. Morton and Deng did not have alibis, but there was nothing beyond slim circumstantial evidence connecting them to the victims." She was reading through the first interview while she talked. Suddenly she asked, "You think this guy has a subtle understanding of karma?" I eyed her a moment, searching for traces of humor. Before I could say anything, she went on. "But it could be a religious thing. We have here three of the four major religions of the world, and Buddhism is the fastest growing."

I shook my head and looked back at the list of victims, then made an ugly "Nah" sound. "This is not religious. It is moral, ethical, philosophical. Our first victim is religiously undefined, the second is an atheist, the third is Jewish, though we don't know if he was practicing, fourth was Judge Jones, a Christian evangelist, fifth was another atheist, and the last was a Buddhist. This has nothing to do with Buddhism, or religion even. These people were killed to make them repent . . ." I trailed off and shook my head. "No, scrub that, not repent. They were killed to make them *aware* of some perceived flaw in their personality. That was the purpose of the music. The only thing Islam wants you to repent for is not converting to Islam, and the only thing you need to be aware of is that there is only one god, and Mohamed is his prophet."

"Harsh," she said absently to the file as she read it. I shrugged. "Find me a mullah who will tell you something different."

"So you don't like Abdo Deng for this?"

I dropped the file on the table, feeling suddenly frustrated and bored. "I wouldn't go that far. It's within the bounds of possibility. But I like Reverend Morton Wells better. What I *really* feel, though, is that Epstein boxed himself into a corner because he got tunnel vision. I think he thought, 'serial killer,' and tried to apply classical serial killer criteria and methodology to the cases. But this is not a standard serial killer, even if such a thing existed."

She sucked her teeth and made a face like I'd put too much sugar in her coffee. "You sure about that?"

I spread my hands wide and sighed. "Standard murder: a relationship is established between K, killer, and V, victim. That relationship gives rise to a motive for killing: K feels jealousy, greed, frustration . . ." I waved my hand in an et cetera. "That motive gives rise to K's desire to kill V, and K acts on that desire. In serial killers that is reversed. The desire to kill arises out of K's psyche for no apparent reason, K then seeks a victim and establishes some kind of relationship, even if just as stalker and prey, and then K kills V. But I don't get the impression that is happening here. I get the impression that our killer connects with these people somehow first, establishes some kind of relationship with them, and from that relationship, from his knowledge of them, arises first the motive, and then the desire, as in a normal murder."

She puffed out her cheeks. "And that motive is?"

"Ethical, philosophical, moral . . . K sees in his victims something that he wants them to reflect on *while* they are in the process of dying. And he, or she, selects the music to stimulate a reflective, spiritual state of mind."

"Jensen was a Buddhist, but K selected Christian music."

The best I could offer to that was, "Hmmm . . ." and then, "Arender was a Jew and he got Tibetan bells."

She looked up at the ceiling. Outside the gray was leaching from the rim of the sky into the dome. Cars were pulling up outside, and there were voices of people greeting each other and laughing. Dehan shook her head at the ceiling.

"Either K doesn't care about denomination, only about spiritual . . ." She spread her hands and shrugged slowly. ". . . merit? Development? Growth? Or, he wants to convert people."

"Cavendish was played Japanese Zen music, Arender had Tibetan bells, and with Georgina Cheng it was . . . Tallis. That makes two out of six non-Christian, and the other four are three Catholic and one Anglican Protestant."

She said, "That feels like a blind alley."

"The whole case feels like a blind alley. I want to start by going to visit Reverend Morton Wells to see if Epstein simply developed a prejudice against him or if there is actually something there. After that we go and talk to Abdo Deng. Meanwhile we need to be getting background on the victims to see how they connect with each other. Somewhere in their background there is some way in which they all connect with each other and with the killer. That much, at least, we can take as a hard fact."

She nodded. "A congregation is a pretty good place to connect with people."

I stood and stretched. "Not if it's a Christian congregation and you aim to meet atheists and Buddhists."

She stood too and touched her toes a couple of times. There was a dog whistle from one of the few desks that were occupied, but she ignored it. I saw who it was and grinned. "Don't try it at home, Alvarez, it's not a good position to get cardiac arrest in, and that Great Dane of yours might get all excited."

"It ain't a Great Dane, wiseass, it's a Doberman!"

"I wasn't talking about your dog. I was talking about your wife."

We left the detectives' room among a barrage of obscenities. As the door closed, I leaned back in. "And, Alvarez? Those little blue pills? They can cause cardiac arrest in a man in your condition."

On the steps outside, dawn had arrived, and it was beginning to smell and sound like morning. I looked at my watch. Eight o'clock was not far off.

Dehan said, "You want to walk? It's twenty minutes, we'll clear our heads."

I nodded, and we made our way through early light down Story Avenue toward Soundview, and the Church of Divine Grace and Rebirth.

THREE

The Church of Divine Grace and Rebirth was a two-story house that had been converted and expanded. It was a flat-fronted building with a flat roof, painted a nasty shade of sickly beige, with peeling red double doors and red bars on the windows. When we arrived the doors were closed, and so were the drapes behind the glass in the windows. I couldn't find a bell, so Dehan hammered with her fist, and while she waited, I took a stroll round back.

Round back was a parking lot with space for maybe a dozen cars, but he also had an area sectioned off behind a fence where he had a garage and a bit of lawn. The garage was open, and I could hear a lot of grunting coming from inside, also an occasional thump. I approached and peered in, unsure what I was going to see.

It turned out to be a man in his late forties or early fifties beating the hell out of a sack he had suspended from the ceiling. You could tell he was in good shape because he was wearing only tracksuit pants and sports shoes. His upper body was that of an athlete, and he moved fast and aggressive, delivering high kicks to the sack that made it quiver and swing. Then he would lay into it with combinations of four, five, and six punches.

I said, "Good morning."

He turned quickly and stared at me. He wasn't exactly hostile, but he wasn't warm and fuzzy either.

"You can't be here. This is my private area. Service is at ten thirty."

I pulled my badge and showed it to him. "The house of the Lord is always open," I said, facetiously, "but not necessarily the house of his minister. Detective John Stone, can you spare a couple of minutes?"

He reached for a towel. "My apologies. As you pointed out, some members of the congregation seem to forget that, where God is divine, His ministers are only human. They expect us to be imbued with the perfection of a deity. How can I help you, Detective?"

I called Dehan, then turned back to the pastor. "Are you Reverend Morton Wells?"

"Yes, I am. Why?"

Dehan appeared at my side and eyed the garage, which was in fact more of a gym, and the reverend.

"Detective Dehan," she said, and showed him her badge. "We were wondering if you would be willing to talk to us about Ana Orcera."

He smiled in a way you could describe as rueful, sighed, and then nodded. "Yes, of course, *again.*" He sat on a bench and gestured us to a plastic chair and another bench. I took the chair, and he said, "What do you want to know? I answered Detective Epstein's questions back in 2015, and since then Sam and I have *almost* become friends."

I returned the smile and nodded. "I know. We genuinely don't want to harass anybody. Detective Dehan and I are the cold-cases unit at the Forty-Third, and the Ana Orcera case has been passed to us. I'm afraid the obvious place to start is . . ."

I gestured at him with my open hand. He was drinking water from a bottle while he listened and watched me. He set the bottle down and dabbed his mouth with a towel.

"I understand. I believe poor Ana's case has been absorbed into a wider case?"

I nodded and offered him a smile as rueful as his own. "What can you tell us about Ana? Detective Epstein was interested in you; we are more interested in Ana. If we can understand her, maybe we can understand how her killer came to select her as a target, and those that followed."

He grunted and stared at the wall awhile, thinking, with the towel hung between his hands. "It's a long time ago, and we were never what you'd call close, despite what Sam Epstein thought. I always thought of her as a lazy, dissolute woman. She was forever either failing to do things she had committed to doing, or she was leaving them half done. I had the impression of a woman who saw her responsibilities as burdens, rather than objectives to be achieved."

Dehan leaned forward with her elbows on her knees, frowning. "Can you put that into context for us? Give us some examples of what you mean . . . ?"

"Yes." He said it like she had asked a question she was going to regret, but now she would have to suck it up. He had his eyebrows raised, and he was nodding. "Yes, I can. She was fat, not grotesquely obese, but definitely overweight to an extent that was unhealthy. She must have promised me, and the congregation, that she was going to tackle that problem a hundred times. Every Sunday she would repeat the promise, but every time I saw her and her son, she was stuffing her mouth with a cake, or a burger, or some item of fast food. I called her out. I called her out *several* times, and she always repeated her promise that she was going to try harder. 'Don't try,' I told her. 'Do it or don't do it. There is no try!'"

Dehan smirked. "Yoda; the Chinese have Confucius, the Europeans have Aristotle and Kant, good old US of A, we have Yoda."

She laughed out loud and slapped her thigh, then punched

me on the shoulder. Wells' smile became strained. "Forgive me," he said. "Yoda?"

I shook my head like it wasn't important. "Oh, a guru-like character from *Star Wars*. He said almost exactly those words to his disciple."

"Oh." When he looked at Dehan again his eyes were cold. "Believe me, I was not quoting from *Star Wars*. I have better authorities than that to quote from."

I ignored the comment and moved on. "So, your overall impression of Ana was of a lazy woman, lacking in will and commitment."

He nodded. "I would say that was a perfect description of her, yes." He paused, reflecting for a moment, and then went on almost apologetically. "The ability to learn places us between the animal kingdom and the divine, but an essential aspect of the ability to learn is the willingness or . . ." He seemed to search his gym for a better word. "The *commitment* to pursue one thought beyond the next, the *desire* to go not merely from A to B, but to follow through then to C and D and perhaps even E!" He sighed. "Ana's son was a consistent underachiever at school. The boy was not particularly stupid, nor was he especially smart. He was average, which meant that with appropriate guidance and teaching, his performance at school might have been slightly above average."

He paused, and I prompted, "But his mother did not help."

He shook his head. "No, she did not, but that is not the point. The point is that she continually came to me, and to the congregation, asking *us* for help. She could not manage her son, she could not get him to do his homework, she could not get him to obey her. So we offered her first advice and then help." He spread his hands. "And she *consistently* failed to take either the advice *or* the help. She had no ability to learn, because she was incapable of taking her failures and using them as lessons." He held out his hand toward me, palm up, as though he was showing me something. "My son has failed in his exams, my pastor and my friends in the congregation are advising me to sit with him an hour a day and help him with homework, and several friends have offered to take him for extra lessons. I will take their advice . . ."

He shook his head. "No, she would weep and moan, beg us for help, and then go right back and make exactly the same mistakes again—and get exactly the same result. The intellectual processes for learning anything but the simplest lessons were missing from her brain."

Dehan pulled a face. "Isn't that what used to be called plain stupid?"

"No. Because when you spoke to her, she was perfectly coherent and perfectly able to understand. She just wasn't able to turn her understanding into learning. She was not stupid, she was lazy. Chronically lazy."

She nodded like that made sense to her. "Can you tell us anything about the kid's father, or any other men in her life?"

"Not very much, Detective Dehan—the boy's father had disappeared long before she joined my congregation. By all accounts he was a waster, a drug addict, and an alcoholic, not to mention a thief. It is a sad fact about certain women that all too often they choose men who hurt them, in many ways, physically, mentally, and spiritually, not to mention morally and financially. And, referring back to my earlier point about Ana, she, like many others, failed to learn and constantly gravitated back to the same kind of man. Shortly before she left my church to join the papist franchise up the road, she had taken in a Sudanese waster who enjoyed getting drunk, smoking pot, and beating her and her son until they could barely walk."

Dehan, suppressing a smile, asked, "Did you ever try to dissuade her from joining the . . ." The grin broke out. "I assume that by 'papist franchise' you mean the Catholic church on Soundview?"

"That's exactly what I mean, and yes, I did indeed try to dissuade her. I even went to her house. Detective, there are two evil religions on this Earth. In my opinion they are truly Satanic, in that they embody all that is evil and dark in the human soul, and they are Catholicism and Islam. They spring from the same desert root, and they both advocate abject prostration and the abdication of choice and personal responsibility. Have you read the Jefferson Bible?"

Dehan shook her head, but I said I had. He went on.

"Then you will realize, Detective Stone, that Jesus' mission in this world was to shine the light of His Holy Grace on a path that led away from the brutality and ignorance of the Old Testament, toward a doctrine of personal responsibility, compassion, and forgiveness. That is what I teach and what I have always believed. When Ana took in that barbarous man and joined the Catholics, I tried very hard to persuade her that she had made a mistake. But it was to no avail. She was lost, and her death was horrible. She did not deserve to die that way. And I confess I have always believed that she died at the hands of her boyfriend."

We sat in silence for a moment. I was thinking hard about what he had said. I glanced at Dehan.

"I'm not sure now what details were released to the press . . ."

He laughed. It was the first time I had seen any sign of humor from him. It seemed to change him into a human being. And that made me think that the overall impression he gave was that of an avenging angel.

"I am quite sure, Detective Stone," he said, "that you remember very well what details were released to the press, and you would love to trip me up on some piece of information that only the killer could possess. But I did not kill Ana. In fact, I pray every day for forgiveness, that I did not do more to save the poor woman.

"What I know is that the killer seems to have been waiting at her house." He shrugged and spread his hands. "Or he was simply *at* her house, where he himself lived, and that shortly after she arrived he broke her arms and legs, stabbed her with a knife, and left her to bleed to death while classical music of some description played in the background. A terrible, barbaric way to die. She must have been in indescribable pain. We can only hope that unconsciousness overtook her soon and she passed out."

"In your opinion, Reverend Wells . . ." I paused for a moment, trying to think of the best way to phrase the question. "In your opinion, was Ana Orcera forgiven because of the way she died?"

The expression on his face told me he thought I was insane.

"*Forgiven?* For what? And by whom?"

"Sloth is a mortal sin. So in Christianity as a whole, she would need forgiveness from God, wouldn't she?"

He rolled his eyes and shook his head. "This is precisely the kind of bullshit that Jesus was trying to get away from. Thomas Aquinas defined sloth as 'sorrow about spiritual good.' He also said that it was a 'sluggishness of the mind' which prevents one from beginning 'good,' which became evil in its *effect* if it drew a man away from performing good deeds. But this is Catholicism, and the Catholics love to take human weakness and turn it into sin."

Dehan surprised me by asking suddenly, "But isn't that *exactly* what sin is? Sin is a daily part of life, because all human beings have human weaknesses. As soon as you hit puberty, you are wanting to sin."

The reverend chuckled. "Dehan, Jewish, right? I like the Jewish view of sin. It is more understanding of the human condition, and ultimately more forgiving. The Catholics got stuck in the Old Testament. It's as though they are forever trying to forget Jesus and his teachings on forgiveness, and they use him only as a symbol of guilt—a cross to beat their followers with. My own view, for what it's worth, is that God is omnipresent and all powerful. That means that He is literally—not figuratively, *literally*—everywhere, and that He is literally able to do *absolutely* everything and anything. Now, you only need to think about this for a fraction of a second to see that all we need in order to achieve forgiveness from God is to know ourselves, *understand* ourselves and our fallibility as humans, and then *forgive ourselves*. His forgiveness is implicit in our own forgiveness, *because* He is omnipotent, *because* He is everywhere, even in our hearts. So, did Ana achieve forgiveness for being lazy? I have no idea, but I hope that as she lay there, bleeding to death and unable to move, she was able to forgive herself for allowing this to happen to her and her son, and then I hope that she forgave her killer."

I nodded slowly a few times. "You have certainly given us a lot to think about. I hope you will forgive *me*, Reverend, but I would be negligent if I did not ask you about your expulsion from the school where you worked, and from your previous church."

He sighed. "It would not be negligent, Detective, because the whole thing is thoroughly documented, and I have been over it numerous times with previous detectives. So everything you need to know is available to you, in your file, without having to ask me. But, you want to see my face and my eyes when you explore the subject."

I nodded. "Yes."

"It was a group of three boys from very privileged WASP families in Manhattan. The school, St. George's Anglican School, as I am sure you know, is in Manhattan. Privilege in this world is inevitable. It happens, and there is nothing we can do about it. But what we *can* do is to ensure, by good education, that privileged children understand the responsibilities that come with privilege. These three boys did not understand their responsibilities toward the rest of society, and I did not miss a single opportunity to draw their arrogance, their conceit, and their bad manners to their attention and that of their parents. I felt it was *my* responsibility. My thanks for my efforts was to be accused by the boys of having molested them sexually. I was summarily dismissed and defrocked. Both the school and the church offered me compensation to the tune of several thousand dollars to keep my mouth shut about what had happened. What had happened was precisely nothing, except that I was accused of something I had not done."

"You accepted?"

"If you've read your file, you know I did. But I think you have lived enough to know, Detective Stone, that there are temporal powers against which we cannot fight. I had lost my career and my future; the least I could do was take their money and try to build a new one of each. I am neither a homosexual nor a pedophile. Nor am I a serial killer, for that matter."

I spread my hands and tilted my head to one side as an expression of apology. "Like I said, I had to ask."

"Detectives, I need to prepare for morning service. Will you catch the killer this time, or is this just another show to be abandoned in the next few days when you hit the same obstacles Epstein did?"

Dehan looked at me with raised eyebrows, perhaps wondering how I would answer. I looked the reverend square in the eye and assured him, "Oh, we'll catch him, you can be very sure of that, Reverend."

He didn't seem real impressed. He stood up and asked us, "Is there anything else?"

Neither of us answered immediately. We watched him a moment and Dehan said, "No, that's about it for now."

And we left.

FOUR

By the time we got back to the station house, the chief was in, watering his bonsai in his office. He always seemed to be watering his bonsai, and I sometimes wondered how much water a bonsai could consume, considering it was a miniature tree. Inspector John Newman set down his miniature watering can and waved us in.

"John, Carmen, please, sit." He sat as we sat. "This case," he added. "Such an odd case. It has been around for six years, and yet . . ." He opened his hands like a man opening a book of blank pages. "Not only have we practically nothing to go on, but not even the press are interested in it. It is too disjointed, there is no continuity of date, sex, victim, apparent motive . . . The only thing that links them—"

"The music," I interrupted, "and not even that has consistency."

"Precisely. So what are we going to do about it?"

"For a start I need a couple of uniforms doing research into the background of each victim. The killer is invisible, but there must be a point where the victims connect, and the killer is sitting on that node."

"Good, fine, you can have O'Connor and Dominguez, I'll tell them to report to your desk. What else?"

"We had a talk with Reverend Morton Wells just now. He was Epstein's prime suspect. I can't say I really formed an opinion except that he seems to be deep, and our killer is definitely deep. I am pretty certain his motivation is at the very least philosophical, if not outright spiritual or religious. This is about . . ." I hesitated, unsatisfied with the word I was going to have to use. "It's about redemption of some kind, or if not redemption, something similar. He is seeking to transform his victims in some way by raising their consciousness as they die."

He frowned at me. In fact, he almost scowled at me. "That is one hell of a statement, John, based on what?"

It was Dehan who answered for me.

"It's the music, sir. The music is different in each case, but it is always sacred music—"

I butted in. "It's music that's used either for Catholic reflection or, in Eastern disciplines, for meditation." I gave a small shrug. "Zen flute music, Tibetan bells, and Tallis from the English Reformation. It is conceivable that the music is just to enhance his own pleasure during the killing, but given the personalized, almost bespoke nature of each murder, I believe the music is chosen very precisely for each victim."

He drew down the corners of his mouth and nodded. "So, if your feeling is correct, we know this much about our killer: that he is a philosopher, he is conversant with sacred music from both the East and the West, and that . . . what? He is seeking to save or redeem lost souls?"

It didn't ring quite true the way he said it, and I was about to tell him it was something like that, but not exactly, when Dehan spoke up again.

"Pretty much, sir, but we still need to find out a lot more. Which is why we want to focus on the victims for now, and their backgrounds. It is still possible that this is a big smoke screen or a red herring. We are also interested in Abdo Deng, a Sudanese refugee who was living with the first victim shortly before she was killed. It seems he may have killed a number of women back in Sudan, though that is as yet unconfirmed. There are allegations that he beat up on the first victim and her son, but we need to confirm that too. And that is about the state of play at the moment."

He'd been taking notes with a Montblanc fountain pen. Now he laid it down and said, "I see. And what about this"—he checked the papers on his desk in front of him—"Reginald Jensen? Can he tell us anything?"

I hopped in before Dehan could get going again. "Obviously we are still waiting on forensics, but preliminary observations are that the victim may have known the killer, because the windows were all closed from the inside, and the lock had not been forced. In fact, that's true of all the victims. There is also the fact that the killer knew that Jensen was inordinately fond of his cat . . ."

"*Inordinately* fond, John? What on Earth do you mean?"

Dehan answered, "He was prepared to give his own life to save the cat, sir."

"Good lord!"

"But that may not have been his fondness for the cat, sir. It may have been an act of devotion, because it seems he was in fact a Buddhist. Either way, the killer knew about Jensen's devotion to his cat, his devotion to Buddhism, or possibly both, and he exploited it in order to kill him. Or, perhaps, he killed him because of his commitment. These are all possibilities and questions we need to address, but we need a lot more factual data, which we can get once we can interview his family or friends."

He nodded and stared down at his fingertips laid along the edge of his desk. "Point taken."

We sat like that for a while until I wondered if he'd gone to sleep, or Bonsai Heaven. Finally he took a deep breath and spoke.

"I am under a lot of pressure to close this case, John. There is never a good time for a serial killer, as I am sure you will both appreciate. But right now, with a tough, uncompromising approach to law and order being *such* a big issue, our political masters at city hall want this dealt with fast."

I looked at him a long time with little expression on my face other than a few blinks. I liked him, he was a good chief, so I didn't want to offend him.

"Sir, I take every case as unique and solve it as quickly and efficiently as I can. If it's a serial killer, then obviously my commitment is even greater because of the risks involved to the public. So, I can't really do it any faster than I would anyway."

He looked embarrassed, and his cheeks actually flushed. He started to say, "Of course not, and I didn't mean . . ."

I interrupted him. "However, if I were to somehow invest more in a case, it would be for the victims and future potential victims, sir. It would not be to satisfy the political anxieties of the political elite. I hope you don't take that amiss, sir."

He swallowed a couple of times. "No," he said, "of course not. Quite right, and I hope you didn't think . . . ummm . . ."

Dehan smiled. "We'll give it our best shot, sir. And we'll bring this bastard in, you can rest assured of that."

"Sooner rather than later," I added, and he nodded and smiled gratefully at us.

We returned to our desks and sat for ten minutes drinking horrible black water and working methodically through the file, compiling what there was on each victim, as a starting point for a more complete victim profile to be built up as the investigation proceeded.

Twenty minutes later, Officers Penny O'Connor, short, red-haired, and freckly, and Javi Dominguez, short, dark, and handsome, both rookies, came into the detectives' room and approached our desk. I gave them the outline of the case and set them the task of building up the profiles of each of the victims, gathering information on family, partners, places where they had lived, and any other details they could dig up, while Dehan tracked down Abdo Deng.

The company he worked for was Union Cars, on the corner

of Castle Hill and Virgil Place. When we called, he wasn't in. His boss explained, "I don't want a goddamn taxi driver who is in my office all day, am I right? I tell 'em: your goddamn car is your goddamn office. If you don't fuckin' like it, go back to fuckin' Eye-rack, or fuckin' Syria, or wherever you fuckin' come from. Am I right?"

When I'd managed to stem the flow of his verbal tide, I said, "Sir, Mr. Deng is not a suspect, I want to stress that, but he may be an important witness. Where can we find him right now?"

"I hope you can find him drivin' his goddamn cab around New York, coz that's what he should be doing right about now."

"What is the number of his taxi."

"Thoity-six."

"Then will you please radio taxicab number thirty-six and tell Mr. Abdo Deng to drop in at the police station on Fteley and Story, as soon as he can?"

"Yah! How's a man supposed to make a buck in this world with the authorities stickin' they fuckin' noses in . . . Yeah, I'll tell him, but don't keep him too long. Time is fuckin' money, remember?"

I hung up before he explained the meaning of life to me, and Dehan said, "Ana had a sister, Carmen."

"Good, do we know where she is?"

Penny O'Connor snapped, "Carmen's Clam Bar, seven seventy-seven Pelham Road. New Rochelle. She owns the joint, only she ain't Carmen Orcera anymore. She's Carmen Jones. Married David Jones, of 4 Greens Way, New Rochelle."

I stood. "C'mon, Carmen Stone, I'll buy you a clam lunch in New Rochelle."

She stood and grabbed her jacket from the back of the chair. "Swell, you think they have hamburgers there, Penny?"

"A whole range of them," said Penny, and flashed sea-green eyes at me that said she would have had clams. How little she understood, I told myself, as Dehan and I stepped out into the midmorn and made our way to the old burgundy beast, which lay basking in the sun on Fteley Avenue.

It was a fifteen-minute drive to New Rochelle. Dehan drove, so we made it in just over ten. We went first to the clam bar and parked outside. It was a curious, one-story, blue-and-white affair with a terrace outside that would have looked more at home in Mexico or the Mediterranean than a small port town ten miles from the border with New England.

We were able to park right outside and, treading over the first few russet leaves of early fall, entered the shabby, blue-and-white eatery. A large woman in her early forties smiled at us with a face that didn't realize it was pretty. She had large brown eyes and a generous mouth. She had been down behind the counter wiping things with a cloth and now stood and fingered a strand of hair from her cheek.

"Good morning! What can I do for you guys? Still warm, but you can feel the chill in the morning!" She added the last bit like maybe she could do something about the chill.

"Nothing you can do about the morning chill," I assured her and smiled, "but we could use a coffee each. I guess it's a bit early for lunch."

She swung around with a big bounce of her ponytail to look at a big old clock on the wall. "Who says?" she cried with a little squeal. "Ten to twelve! I can fix yous a preprandial martini with an olive and a pickled onion to open up your appetites, while I prepare you some clams, and meanwhile you can be studying the menu for your main course!"

Dehan was smiling at me like she thought I was somehow funny. I ignored her and spoke to the delightful Carmen.

"I would love to take you up on that, but we will have to forego the martinis because we are on duty."

She clapped her hands together in front of her bosom and bent her knees to make a little bob. "You're *cops*? Oh-my-*good-Lord*! And here I am chattering on about clams and martinis!"

We showed her our badges and introduced ourselves and then

told her we'd have some clams simmered in white wine and then a homemade King Burger with homemade Cayenne-Catsup. When we'd told her that, I said, "And, I am guessing that you are Carmen Jones, née Orcera . . ."

She blinked at me and then blinked at Dehan, then back at me again. "Yes," she said simply. "Why?"

"Carmen, we are actually here to talk about your sister."

Her eyes went wide, and she stared hard at me. "Did he confess? Did you finally catch the son of a bitch?"

I arched an eyebrow, but Dehan leaned on the counter with both elbows and asked, "Who, Carmen? Did who confess?"

Suddenly the large, pretty face was flushed with anger, her eyes were bright, and her cheeks were aflame.

"That bastard Abdo Deng! I swear! You keep me away from him because if I *ever* get my hands on him, Lord!" She waved a finger at me. "Give me patience and not strength for I *swear—I swear!*—if you give me strength I will *tear* his head clean off his shoulders!"

"Well, that's interesting." Dehan smiled at me. "Ain't it?"

I said, "Carmen, can you spare us ten minutes, to explain that?"

"I'll give you more than ten minutes. We don't get busy for another hour." She leaned back, staring down the counter at the kitchen door. "*David!*" she bellowed in a huge voice, "*I'm going to talk to the cops!*"

David appeared in the kitchen door with a bewildered face and his thin shoulders hunched. "Hell, honey, all I said was . . ." He stopped, staring at us. I held up my badge. "Detectives John Stone and Carmen Dehan."

He smiled, showing most of his teeth, and nodded at his wife. "Okay, sweetheart. I'm right here if you need me . . ."

She poured herself a beer from the tap, and we followed her to a table out on the terrace. There she sat with a grunt and a sigh and drew off half of the beer while we sat and watched. As she wiped away the foam with the back of her hand, I asked again,

"So, what makes you believe that it was Abdo Deng who killed your sister?"

She raised her eyes in a way that said she didn't really believe what she was hearing. "He *told* me! I told the detective at the time. And I never could understand why that slimy bastard Abdo was never arrested. Though, tell you the truth, I was not all *that* surprised. That detective never did really listen to me. He was one of those 'little lady' guys." She turned to Dehan. "Know what I mean? Always patronizing you and putting you down, like you don't know what the hell you're talking about. I told him! I *told* him, 'I been running a successful business for ten years. How long have you been running your own business, wiseass?' I called him that, wiseass. I told him all right. But he still didn't listen."

Dehan pressed her, "What, Carmen? What did Abdo tell you?"

"I can even remember his name, after all these years, Epstein, like the scientist, Albert Epstein."

I nodded. "Sam Epstein. What did Abdo say to you, Carmen?"

"He *told* me," she said heavily, laboring each word, "and I told that cop, Epstein, that he'd said he was going to kill Ana! Abdo Deng told me he was going to kill my sister Ana."

FIVE

"ABDO DENG TOLD YOU HE WAS GOING TO KILL YOUR sister?" It was Dehan, she was leaning forward with her palms on the edge of the table.

"Straight to my face, closer than you're sitting now. Only he was standing, and we were at the door of her house in Clason Point. He says to me, 'You better understand, you tell your bitch sister she is not with some American *khawal khara*!' I can still hear his nasty voice saying the words right now. I looked them up . . ."

"*Khawal khara?*"

"Some American shit nancy. I don't speak Arabic and I don't care to, but that stuck in my mind, so I will never forget it. 'Tell her she's not with some shit nancy American now, she is with a real Arab man who knows how to treat an American *eahira!*' That's a whore in Arabic. I looked that up too."

"That's disgusting," said Dehan, "but it's not a death threat."

"No, when he was done calling American men nancies and American women whores, he pulled a switchblade from his pants and flicked it open in my face, and he says, 'Tell her, if she gives me any more trouble, I will cut her open from her womb to her throat.' I tell you I went cold inside. The *look* on his face made your blood run cold in your veins. It was *evil*! It was just plain *evil*!"

I frowned. "What was the argument about? I'm guessing they had a row, you were there, and you took him aside . . ."

"Oh," she interrupted me, waving both hands in my direction, "it was one of many, *many* rows! Dad was Spanish, from Spain, and Mom Italian from Italy, and they were both very liberal—in the old sense of the word." She laughed and leaned on Dehan's arm. "The kind of liberals who thought it was *good* to offend people, not this bunch of . . . Anyhow, so we both grew up real clear that women were not put on this Earth to cook for men and bear their babes. But this piece of *mierda*, as my dad would say, would spend all day sitting on the couch playing video games and then, when Ana came in from work, he'd start, 'Make food, clean the house, this place is like a pigsty, my mother would be ashamed if she knew where I lived . . .' But this particular time he had gone too far. He told her he would be better off using her and her sister—me—as whores, at least we would make some money for him. Well, Ana had had enough, she went for him, and he started beating on her. I hit him with a vase. He gave me a couple of backhanders, and Ana dialed 911. He said he was leaving. I guess she hung up, and I pushed him to the door. That was when he said what he said."

Dehan drew breath to ask a question, but I beat her to it. "You said, 'when Ana came in from work . . .' What work was that?"

Carmen sighed and slumped back in her chair with a smile on her face that wasn't exactly a happy one.

"Thing is, me and Carmen, in many ways we were very similar. When we were kids, people thought we were twins sometimes. But there was one big difference in our characters. I am all go, go, go. What do we need to do? This! Right! Let's do it! She, honestly, was about as lazy as they come. Like him. You go in there sometimes and there'd be three-day-old pizza cartons on the floor, empty beer bottles, the beds unmade . . . It was real sad and a bad environment for a kid to grow up in. So she had part-time jobs here and there, and sometimes they'd have a little more money. But that bastard never contributed nothing to the home. It was all her, her, her. I don't know what he did with his money. He sure as hell didn't give it to Ana."

Dehan asked now, "How long before her death was the fight, Carmen?"

She shook her head. "Not long, not long at all, and I'll tell you why." She pointed at me. "I'll tell you why," she repeated. "It was that row, when she heard the threat he made about her, that made her kind of reassess her life. We was brought up Catholics. I can't say I am devout, but I am sincere. But Ana was forever looking for the easy answer, the easy way out." She turned to Dehan. "Know what I mean? Always looking for a quick fix, salvation now with no effort. And when she saw that her life, and her son's, were in real, actual danger, she realized how far—just how far—she had strayed from the path. And she decided to reform. So she left that . . ."—she waved her finger in the general direction of New York City—"that child molester's sect on Leland Avenue and returned to her own faith, let's face it, the only *real* church, the Catholic Church, Mother Church." She paused, looking down at her hands laid on the table to either side of her beer. "Just a couple of days after that she was dead. I still haven't really come to terms with it."

We didn't talk for a moment. She was back with her sister, seeing her face and hearing her voice, and I wondered if she might remember something more. So I didn't speak. Suddenly she smiled, gave a small laugh, and shook her head.

"I'll say one thing, she was forever searching, forever seeking."

"Seeking what?" Dehan asked, sharing her smile.

She gave her head a couple of big shakes. "Damned if I know. An answer? An easy way out? An explanation that made sense? A reason for all the pain? She went through Yoga, Tao, Buddhism, a different kind of Buddhism in Shorehaven, Gospel, Methodism . . ." She shook her head again in tired disbelief at what she was remembering. "Then there was the weird stuff. Every now and then she would get involved with some kind of cult: Wicca, Crowley, UFOs—she thought they were going to come and save us, and hooked up with some guy who channeled an alien god . . . Hell, the list just went on and on. Not many things lasted more than a few weeks."

Dehan was looking interested. "How long did she last at the Church of Divine Grace and Rebirth?"

"Creepy Morton?" She nodded. "No, she was with him a long time. Couple of years at least. And I have to tell the truth"— she put her right hand on her left breast to show she was telling the truth—"he did help her. For a while there she started cleaning herself up, looking respectable, taking the kid to school on time and collecting him on time, doing part-time jobs, saving a bit of money. But then she met Abdo, and it all came to an end."

"Were she and Morton Wells lovers?"

She pulled the corners of her mouth down and shrugged. It was an expression that said this was not the first time she had wondered about it.

"She was easy, and he's a pervert, so your guess is as good as mine."

I asked, "Did he visit her much?"

"I have to be honest. I don't know. I am only aware of one time he ever visited her, and that was a few days before she died. She told me he was real mad at her for leaving the church, and especially for hooking up with Abdo. She said she'd told him, the reverend, that she'd broken it off with him. But the rev didn't believe her. He thought she'd left his church because of Abdo, which was a bit crazy seeing as Abdo was a Muslim, and she'd gone back to Catholicism. And he also accused her of sacrificing her child's future and his happiness on the altar of her own egotism, sloth, and vanity. I remember those words."

She suddenly put her hand to her forehead. "Would you look at me? You two beautiful people ordered your lunch a *century* ago, and here I am sitting here talking my head off about nonsense! Let me go and tell David to get those orders going!"

She went to stand, but Dehan stopped her.

"Carmen, we are here for your sister. She has been six years waiting for justice, and we mean to bring it to her—and her killer. The lunch is just a pleasant bonus."

"I understand . . ."

I cleared my throat. "For my part, I have only one more question before lunch." I smiled at her. "You have talked a lot about her son. You haven't mentioned his name or where he is now. Do you often see him?"

"Bartolome, or Bartholomew as he is now. He became a very troubled, angry child. We adopted him, so at least he had the stability of staying in the same family. He saw a psychiatrist for a long while, and now he boards at a private school that specializes in troubled kids. We agonized over the decision for a long time, but in the end we decided it was best. We see him every weekend and every holiday. But at the school he has a counselor, a psychologist, and above all routine, routine, routine, and discipline." She winced up at the sky and hesitated a moment. "He was at school the day she was killed, and we collected him from school. He doesn't know anything, any details; I would really prefer that you didn't question him."

I nodded. "We'll try our best to avoid it if it's not necessary."

She nodded, got up, and went to the kitchen to give our order to her husband. Dehan and I sat staring at each other in silence. People often felt uncomfortable when we did that, but it helped us think, like we were having a silent conversation. Eventually she sighed and looked down at her thumbs in her lap.

"Okay, here's the thing. I don't like Reverend Morton Wells. I think he's pedantic, I think he's an ego freak, and my gut tells me he has no conscience. But does my gut tell me he's a serial killer who murdered Ana Orcera . . . ?" She puffed out her cheeks and made a very expansive gesture with her hands. "What can I tell you?"

"On the other hand . . ."

"On the other hand, Abdo Deng, he just keeps ticking all the boxes."

"I don't like the man Carmen described any better than you do. But we are cops, Dehan, and we have to remember that we deal in facts. We have not, as yet, met Abdo Deng. We have only heard two people's opinions about him. So it's those opinions that are ticking boxes right now, not him."

"Okay, big guy, wrist slapped, now let's both deal with the fact that we both know that bastard is exactly as he has been described."

I sighed. "Perhaps, but even if he is as described, I think you are losing sight of something."

"Tell me, guide me, Sensei, give me light where I am blind." She said all that with a flat voice and no facial expression.

"You are losing sight of the fact that Abdo Deng is ticking the boxes of a stereotypical woman killer. He appears to be a misogynistic, violent bully. But four of our six victims are men."

She grunted and shook her head. "He may be misogynistic, but he is *also* a bully, and by the sounds of it, even if he is not on a jihad, he certainly seems to have strong anti-Western feelings. Now, O Wise One, note this: victim number two, an atheist, a philanthropist, and a financier, so probably weak . . ."

"A monstrous, unfounded generalization, but proceed, Little Grasshopper."

She snapped her fingers and shook her head. "You're right, I forgot about all those brawling Vikings on Wall Street, quaffing ale and hitting each other with axes. Shut up and stop interrupting."

"Fine."

"Third victim, Saul Arender, Jewish, an attorney, and however passionate, intense, and aggressive he may be as a defense attorney, he probably had six ulcers, enough cholesterol in his arteries to pad a whale, and blood pressure up in the two hundreds."

Carmen emerged from the restaurant with two large, foaming beers and set them in front of us.

"It was two beers you asked for, right? The clams will be another ten minutes."

She hurried away and Dehan shrugged. "Two coffees does sound a bit like two ice-cold foaming beers, and it would be rude to send them back. The poor woman has been through enough. Besides, I think I heard her say they were alcohol free."

My only response was a blink while she pulled off half the glass, sighed, belched softly, and wiped her mouth with the back of her hand. I sipped my own beer and said, "You were saying about the Vikings on Wall Street."

"Yeah, fourth victim, Judge Jeremiah Jones, known affectionately as Three Jay, a revolutionary evangelist with very progressive ideas about Eastern religions. Also a man with enough cholesterol to supply the world with biodiesel for the next hundred years.

"Sixth and final victim, a Buddhist and a physically weak man. So each male victim ticks two important boxes: the men are physically weak, and they have strongly held religious views which are anathema to Islam. Bully and fundamentalist."

I thrust out my lower lip and nodded ponderously.

"You make a powerful point, Little Grasshopper."

"Not only that, big guy, but it actually opens up an interesting new perspective."

"It does?"

"That his preferred victim is a man who has strayed from the true path, or has rejected it. Hence the suggestion of retribution and guidance back to the truth, whereas women are merely to be punished. Ana with her bones broken, Georgina Cheng badly mutilated. Islam, like Christianity, places a lot of emphasis on repenting for rejecting God before you die." She gave her head a twitch and picked up her beer. "My gut is telling me he's the guy."

I nodded for a while, until the smell of white wine and clams drew me out of my reverie. Carmen set down our plates, knives, forks, and spoons, and the steaming bowl in the middle of the table. We made appreciative—and frankly sincere—"ooh" and "aaah" noises, and, after a bob and a giggle, she went away tossing her ponytail. Dehan scooped succulent shellfish onto her plate with an alluring rattle, and as I watched her I said, "You make a very compelling argument, Archie."

She chuckled. "Archie, now?"

"It seems appropriate, with the clams . . ."

"And the beer."

"And the beer."

"But?"

I shook my head and leaned forward to help myself to some shellfish, and doused them with the white wine sauce. "No buts. It is a little premature, especially considering we haven't even seen the man yet, but you do make a very compelling case."

I picked up my glass, and we toasted, and then drank deep, like those Wall Street Vikings.

SIX

By the time we'd finished our early lunch, Abdo Deng had still not shown at the 43rd. So I telephoned Union Cars.

"What do you want from me? I called him. Now he's not answering his phone. Lazy foreign bastard has taken my taxi and he's done a bunk. If he has stolen my taxi, I'll sue the city. See? This is what I get for trying to be a good citizen and cooperate with the cops!"

I hung up. "He's gone AWOL."

She took her cell from her jacket. "I'll put out a BOLO on him and his cab. But if he's done a runner, he'll dump the cab pretty soon. Two gets you twenty he has another bus parked somewhere."

"No doubt we'll find out soon enough. Let's get back to the station. I want to take Penny off victims and put her on Abdo Deng. I want to know everything there is to know about him."

I stood and held out my hand. She tossed me the keys and narrowed her eyes. "Why Penny?"

"Bejaysus, hasn't she got the most wild Irish eyes you ever did see, after all? And amn't I all bewitched by them and helpless all the same?"

She made a dismissive noise and stood. "She's about as Irish as I am. And that goes for your accent too, by the way."

"That may be so, Dehan, but she is also a little more awake and snappy than Mr. Dominguez."

We bid our farewells and climbed into the old Jag, then headed back along Pelham Shore Road, across the Split Rock golf course, toward the Bronx.

Back at the 43rd I parked on Fteley Avenue, and we climbed the shallow steps and made our way to the detectives' room. As we approached our desks, Penny jumped to her feet and addressed Dehan.

"Detective, I was looking into the second victim, Mathew Cavendish? He had a son. That doesn't appear in the file. The boy is now sixteen, which means he was about twelve at the time of his father's murder."

"Good work, O'Connor. Anything else?"

"Yeah, he currently lives with his grandparents on West Eighty-Eighth. Five-story, double-fronted house. The kid attends The Holy Trinity, a Catholic boys' school on West Ninety-First."

Dehan looked at me and said, with unreasonable asperity, "Convenient, short walk from home. Saves on gas."

I nodded. "Good. Dominguez, I want you to focus on Cavendish and his family and friends now. See what you can find out about anyone who might have had a grudge, and pay special attention to his religious beliefs, any clubs or sects he may have belonged to at any time. But don't get bogged down. Get what you can, then move on to Saul Arender."

He listened carefully and nodded. "You got it, Detective."

O'Connor handed him her notes, and I steered her back toward her seat. "You I want to focus on Abdo Deng. Where, precisely, did he come from? How long has he been here? Who did he come with? Where are they now? Has he got a record back in Sudan? Has he got a record here? Married, kids, parents, grandparents, aunts, uncles, cousins, bank accounts? Absolutely everything."

"I'll get on that right away, Detective." She didn't click her heels and salute, but it felt like she wanted to. Dehan was holding a piece of paper O'Connor had given her and was dialing with her left thumb. We stared at each other while it rang, and she chewed her lip. Then she looked at the floor and said, "Good afternoon, this is Detective Carmen Dehan of the New York Police Department. Is that Mrs. Cavendish?" She nodded a few times while she listened, then, "Mrs. Cavendish, we are a cold-case unit working out of the Forty-Third Precinct, and we are investigating the murder of your son, Mathew, back in 2016. Would it be convenient for us to come and see you this afternoon . . . ?" She glanced at her watch. "Yeah, that would be fine, thank you." She hung up. "They'll be home all afternoon, and only too glad to help us. Mat Senior will be writing his memoirs in his den but will take a break to come and talk with us."

I nodded absently, looking down at the file, open on the desk. "I don't often bet, Dehan, as you well know. But I am going to lay a bet with you." I pointed down at the open pages. "Our only suspects so far are a Muslim who might be a jihadist, and a defrocked reverend with his own church; our first victim is a lapsed Catholic who tried every religion under the sun, and some beyond it; and our last victim is a Buddhist. We have been told that Mathew Cavendish was an atheist, but I am willing to bet twenty bucks that he had at some point in the past started to take an interest in Buddhism."

She frowned. "Why? That seems pretty thin, Stone."

I ignored the comment and turned to Dominguez. "Check Cavendish's bank records. See if he made any donations to any religious organizations, or if he was a member of any kind of religious or philosophical society."

Dehan was frowning down at the names. "You think the connection might be religion? Wow, that's out there . . . Three Jay was evangelical, but Cheng was an atheist. Saul Arender was Jewish, but we don't know if he was practicing or not . . . I don't know, Stone."

I shrugged "Course, if you're too chicken . . ."

She snorted. It was a derisive sound. "Okay, who are the victims whose religion we do not know about?"

It was Dominguez who answered. "Victims one and two we know about; as you just pointed out, Detective Stone, Orcera was a lapsed Catholic with fluctuating interests. She had returned to the church just before she died, and Mr. Cavendish was a committed atheist. Saul Arender was Jewish by birth and education, and he still attended the synagogue from time to time. Judge Jeremiah Jones was an evangelist but an unusual one; he had a real interest in Eastern philosophies and often talked and wrote about how the West could benefit from a deeper understanding of Eastern philosophy."

I arched an eyebrow at him. "How'd you happen to know that, Dominguez?"

He glanced at Penny O'Connor and smiled. "Oh, we've been doing a preliminary survey of each person prior to an in-depth study, in case there was something urgent we should communicate to you."

"Huh." I nodded. "So that leaves Georgina Cheng . . ."

"Atheist, known for commenting on TV and radio that she believed religion was a curse on humanity."

"And Jensen . . ."

"A practicing Buddhist, Detective, and a member of his local vihara on Cornell Avenue. So we pretty much know about all their religious views, at least at a superficial level . . ."

Dehan shrugged at me. "We're going over beaten ground. We already said, we have one Catholic, two atheists, one Jew, one evangelist, and one Buddhist."

I smiled at her. "Yeah, that wasn't my point, but never mind. Let's see how it plays out. Bet or no bet?"

She rolled her eyes but laughed. "Fine! Twenty bucks says he was a plain old atheist."

"Twenty bucks says he was at the very least interested in Buddhism."

I spat in my palm, and we shook.

WEST 88TH STREET cuts across the Upper West Side of Manhattan from the Jacqueline Kennedy Onassis Reservoir, in Central Park, to the Soldiers' and Sailors' Memorial on Riverside Drive. About halfway down the last block, around the three hundreds, is an elegant terrace of handsome four-story Victorian houses, complete with stoop and basement that you could probably snap up for anything between several million and a few million more.

I found a space outside the Cavendish home, and Dehan bounded up the stoop and rang on the bell while I locked the car. As I followed her up the eleven steps to the porch, she turned and pointed at me.

"We need an old brownstone, with a stoop and huge rooms on the inside with stained glass and marble fireplaces."

"Is that so? And what do we need that for?"

"Because that is the way we are supposed to live . . ."

"You and I?"

"Yes, just that the memo went astray and we wound up in Morris Park."

I jutted out my bottom lip. "Oh, it's not so bad."

"But it's not a brownstone on the Upper West Side."

"No, it's not that."

"I see you there, in slippers, with a blue cardigan and a pipe, tapping your cold cases out on a typewriter."

She giggled, and I smiled. "You know what you can do, don't you?"

I was spared having to tell her by the opening of the large, oak door behind her. There was a young woman there who had an indefinable European air and looked like she'd been reared on double cream and tulips. She said, "Hello," and smiled a smile forged in cornfields while yodeling.

We showed her our badges. "Detectives Stone and Dehan, we're here to see Mr. and Mrs. Cavendish."

"Oh yah, please to follow, I will show you the way."

We followed her across an entrance hall that was about the size of my living room and decorated in highly polished mahogany and brass, a couple of dark green armchairs that looked like antiques, and muted, amber lighting from wall lamps set in oak-paneled walls, to a set of heavy, dark double doors that led into a comfortable living room that was more lived in than elegant. There was an overstuffed calico sofa and a couple of vast armchairs in the same material all ranged around a fireplace that right then sported a vase of dried chrysanthemums but showed clear signs of being lit regularly through the winter months. There was no coffee table to graze your shins on, but every seat had at least one lamp table where you could set your whiskey or your cup of coffee while staring at the flames. There was no TV visible, but there was an old record player and a huge collection of vinyls. The books, an eclectic mix of paperbacks and hardbacks, flanked the fireplace and filled long, low, blond wood bookcases along the walls and must have numbered two thousand at least.

There was a man in his late sixties, with steel-gray hair, standing by the fireplace, and a woman perhaps ten years younger than him sitting on the sofa, turned slightly to watch us come in. Our European guide said, "Detectives Dehan and Stone to see you."

The man nodded at her, said, "Thank you, Yolanda," and advanced toward me with his hand held out. We shook, and he said, "Mathew Cavendish; this is my wife, Hazel."

I made our introductions, and he gestured us to the sofa and the armchairs. "You don't mind if I stand. I spend most of the time sitting these days, writing my memoirs. To be honest, I thought our son's case had sunk without a trace."

I sat in the armchair, facing Cavendish and his wife. Dehan took a seat next to her on the sofa.

"Sometimes," I said, "cases do go cold. You can only go as far as the evidence takes you with a case before you risk slipping into unethical practices. But we do have a unit at the Forty-Third that specializes in taking cold cases and having a fresh look at them. But your son's case is not exactly cold. It is part of a broader, ongoing investigation."

He frowned. "Really? I am not sure I follow. What broader investigation?"

Dehan made a rueful smile and answered. "Well, in a sense, that is what we are trying to work out. You see, we have a series of victims . . ."

Hazel Cavendish spoke for the first time. "Murder victims?"

"Yes, murder victims, who apparently have nothing in common except that they appear to have been killed by the same man."

Cavendish grunted down at his shoes. "So, basically, what you are telling us is that you are trying to connect these victims somehow." He looked up at me, as though he had startled himself with a thought. "Somehow, that is, aside from the modus operandi of your putative killer."

I nodded. "That's about the size of it for now."

"So you still have no idea who did this, or why."

"It's perhaps not quite as hopeless as that sounds," I said. "Since we took over the case, certain patterns have come to light that were not obvious before, and we certainly have people we are interested in. But we need to be methodical and thorough."

Hazel Cavendish said, "What is it you want to know?"

I smiled at her. "It may surprise you."

Her laugh was a tired, only slightly amused gasp. "That would be a nice change. I'm afraid I am not easily surprised these days."

I nodded that I understood and said, "I understand that Mathew was an atheist, is that correct?"

Cavendish exploded, "My God! You don't mean to tell me . . . !"

"Not"—I raised my hand, palm out, to stop him—"not exactly, please let me explain. We do not believe that he was killed because he was an atheist. That would be totally inaccurate. But, having said that, one of our lines of inquiry suggests that the murder might be related to religion in some way."

He sighed, went up on his toes, and looked around the room, licking his lips.

"Son," he said at last, "that might make a lot of sense to you, but to me you're talking gibberish. Either he was killed because of his religious views or he wasn't."

"The simple answer, Mr. Cavendish, is that we don't know. But what we can say is that it seems there may be a connection with religion in the killer's mind."

Mrs. Cavendish snorted. "That should not surprise us, after all. There has been no greater cause of untimely death in this world than religion, and in particular the Abrahamic family of religions. Their obsession with monotheism, subservience, and obedience. There is no sin but disobedience to God—look at the story of Abraham, ordered to kill *his own son*, Isaac! And in abject obedience to this monstrous order, Abraham builds an altar and prepares to kill him. And this, *this* is the lesson we teach our children day after day: abject obedience is good, disobedience is sin!"

"Hazel." His voice was quiet, but it carried authority. She glanced at him, then looked away. "Forgive me for saying so, Detective, but it doesn't seem to be a lot to go on . . ."

Dehan cut across him. "We are not at liberty to discuss the details of our investigation, Mr. Cavendish. But we are doing the best we can with a very difficult case. What we are looking for is just a few answers to help us understand what happened to Mathew, and whether it did, in fact, have anything to do with his views on religion."

He smiled at her. "I shall consider myself suitably told off, Detective Dehan. What do you want to know?"

She glanced at me. I said, "Was Mathew always an atheist?"

He raised his eyebrows high and pulled down the corners of his mouth. I saw Hazel turn and glare at him. He started to speak. "Atheism is an intellectual stance, Detective. It is the product of reflection and analysis. Can a boy of ten who professes to be an atheist, but who has done none of the necessary analyses or reflection, truly be said to be an atheist . . . ?"

"You know perfectly well, Mathew." Hazel snapped the words out like double taps from a semiautomatic. "That your son was perfectly well equipped by the age of eight to understand the basic, core concepts of religion and to make an informed decision before he was ten!"

Cavendish drew breath to answer, but I got in first. "Did he explore any religions other than the Abrahamic ones? Some Oriental religions are more like philosophies . . ."

Cavendish looked at his wife and gestured to her with an open hand. "Would you like to answer this, dear?"

"Naturally, he explored Taoism, Hinduism, and Yogi philosophies as well as Zen Buddhism, Tibetan Buddhism, and classical Theravada Buddhism, and Shinto of course."

"He was deeply interested in the subject, obviously."

Her jaw jutted out slightly, as though I were challenging her somehow. "Utterly fascinated, and from a very early age."

"So, his study of these other religions and philosophies, was it limited to reading at home, or did he actively . . ."

She was already shaking her head. "No, he was very independent. He was not a joiner, he never belonged . . ."

"Hazel!"

We all looked at him, except Hazel. There was more sadness in his eyes than anger, but his expression was stern.

"Hazel, you cannot—you *may not*—project your own being, your own way of being in the world, onto Mathew. He was his own man and had his own way of doing things. You should be proud of that!" She looked away, and he sighed. To me he said, "Some years ago, it must have been a couple of years before he died, Mathew became very interested in an early branch of Buddhism . . ."

"Theravada."

He looked pleasantly surprised. "Why, yes. He was fascinated by it, as am I even today, but Hazel disapproves. Anyway, he went so far as to join the vihara and sign up for several courses. For a very brief period of maybe a year . . ."

"The *longest* year of my life!" interposed Hazel.

"He said that he might seriously consider becoming a Buddhist. But in the end he decided against it. As he said, Buddha was not a Buddhist."

I looked at Dehan and smiled sweetly at her. "But Mathew Cavendish, briefly, very nearly was."

SEVEN

Cavendish glanced at us curiously, seemed to dismiss it, and plowed on.

"Buddhism, as a philosophy rather than a religion, manages to sidestep the pseudo-academic nightmare, contradictions and paradoxes of subjectivism and objectivism that result from the completely false dichotomy of empiricism and rationalism, by stating, 'everything is mind.'"

Hazel's voice came as a drawl. "Mathew . . . You are boring our guests."

He barely paused for breath before answering. "They are not guests, dear. They are investigators who are"—he smiled at us, pleased with himself, as though he had set the whole thing up on purpose—"who are," he repeated, "rather pleasingly, searching for the truth. It is as though karma itself had taken a hand . . ."

I thought I had better cut him short before he got into his stride and slipped in, "A defense attorney once told me that there is no place in the law for the truth. Truth is an abstract, philosophical concept. The law is only interested in facts, and facts are things you can prove in court, with evidence, before a judge and a jury. I'm afraid there is not much room for philosophy in a murder inquiry, Mr. Cavendish."

"Here," said Mrs. Cavendish suddenly, "I am afraid I am with my husband. You are dealing with issues of life and death. How much more fundamental can you get? We are talking about the existence of a person, and another person's ethical right to *take away that person's very existence.* Surely, if truth is present anywhere, it is in the act of killing another person."

I suppressed a small sigh and offered her a smile that said I was tired and wanted to get back to work.

"With all due respect, Mrs. Cavendish, I have no doubt that you are right, but where you are talking about the truth inherent in one person's killing another, I am talking about the forensic *facts* attached to one person's *murdering* another. Life and death are part of truth; murder is a crime contrary New York Penal Law one twenty-five and subsections thereof. Death is mystical transition, perhaps. Murder is a breach of the law. And *that* is what we are talking about."

They glanced at each other, but before they could start philosophizing again, I changed the subject.

"Your grandson, where is he now?"

She answered, glancing at her watch. "He is at school. He will be collected by friends. We did not want him to have to face the ordeal of remembering. We will collaborate with you in every way, but if you want to talk to him, you will have to get a court order, and we will contest it. There is nothing he can tell you that we can't."

"That's one hell of a statement, Mrs. Cavendish, particularly in view of the fact that we are looking for your son's killer."

"Murderer, according to you." There was a flicker in her eye that said she'd regretted the comment the moment she'd made it. I went to speak, but Dehan, frowning, beat me to it.

"I'm a little confused. I assumed, when we came here, that we would be on the same side, aiming to achieve the same thing. But I am picking up some hostility." She looked at me. "Am I wrong?" She looked at them in turn. "You don't want your son's killer caught?"

She looked at Mrs. Cavendish, defying her with her eyes to correct the statement again. Hazel closed her eyes and sighed.

"There is no hostility, Detective. Mathew's death was extremely traumatic for Grant. He is slowly coming to terms with it. To rake it all up again now would be nothing less than catastrophic."

Mathew cleared his throat and added, "You know his mother died just a couple of years before his father did. If we hadn't been granted custody, I don't know what would have happened to him."

"And then . . ." It was Hazel, but her husband snapped a look at her and she turned away, biting her lip.

"And then what?" I said.

"They need to know, Mathew!"

He covered his face with his hands. "*Hazel!* Why can you not *learn* to keep your mouth *shut*?"

Dehan rolled her eyes at me. "Whatever the answer is, Mr. Cavendish, now it's too late. So, and then, what? What happened?"

He sighed heavily. "Even though Mathew was an atheist, like a lot of atheists he acknowledges that religious schools have a considerably higher standard of education than nondenominational ones, especially Catholic and traditional Anglican ones. There is more discipline, more sense of purpose and direction."

"And . . . ?"

"From the age of four, until his father was murdered in 2016, Grant attended St. George's Anglican School for Boys."

Dehan stared at me a moment, then said, "And that was the school where there was a scandal because one of the teachers was accused of abusing the children."

"That's right. We were never able to find out whether Grant had been molested or not. He never spoke about anything like that. He seems happy and secure, though he still has occasional nightmares about his father. But we are committed to protecting him, whatever it takes."

I nodded. "We understand that. I'd like you to understand that we are committed to that too. We won't do anything to hurt Grant..."

Cavendish smiled ruefully and supplied the missing words I had been reluctant to utter.

"Unless it is absolutely necessary."

I stood. "Unfortunately, Mr. Cavendish, when men make institutions like the law, those institutions acquire a life of their own, and they are quite indifferent to their creators' emotional needs. We made the law blind and impartial, as you know. But I can promise you that we, Detective Dehan and I, as people, will do our best to spare Grant any unnecessary anxiety."

They didn't thank me. They just watched me, and we left.

Down in the street I leaned on the warm, burgundy roof of my Jag and drummed a tattoo with the butt of my key. Dehan rested her butt on the hood and stared at me.

"Truth," I said.

"Dare," she answered, and winked.

"Most philosophy students, and most academic philosophers, are not really concerned with finding the truth—or the 'Truth,' with a capital *T*. Most students of philosophy and their teachers are concerned with either asking questions that are impossible to answer or criticizing other philosophers' attempts to answer those questions."

"Like an ongoing navel-gazing convention."

"But this guy . . ." I drummed some more tattoos and gazed up at the Great Navel in the Sky. "This guy is different. He is looking for an answer. The right answer *is*, by definition, the truth, right?"

She shrugged. "Sure, if it wasn't, it would be a lie, or a mistake. If it's the right answer, then it is the truth, yeah. Where is this getting us?"

I didn't answer for a long time, sucking my teeth and staring along the straight, leafy line of West 88th Street.

"It's getting us," I said at last, "inside the head of our killer.

He wants the truth, but not just anyhow. He wants it in a very particular way."

She bunched her lips into a straight line and shook her head. "Sorry, big guy, I have no idea what you are talking about."

I arched an eyebrow at her. "You owe me twenty bucks."

She looked startled. "What? Why? What for?"

"I quote," I said: "'Twenty bucks says he was a plain old atheist.' To which I replied, 'Twenty bucks says he was at the very least interested in Buddhism.' Then I spat in my palm, and we shook. That seals a bet, Dehan, as you well know. Therefore . . ."

I held out my hand, palm up. She rolled her eyes, pulled her wallet from her back pocket, and slapped twenty bucks in my hand.

"Okay, Sensei, so he was interested in Buddhism, but what struck me *a lot* more forcefully than that was the fact that Cavendish's son had been at the St. George's Anglican School."

"That was a surprise, and it is a significant connection between two of the victims . . ."

"I can feel a however coming."

I arched an eyebrow at her. "I can think of several answers to that, and they are all rude. Try to stay on track, Dehan. The thing is, that particular connection is not one that is likely to repeat itself with the other four."

She made a "should I slap you now or leave it for later" face. "Come on, Stone! Sure, Saul Arender, Judge Jones, Georgina Cheng, and Reginald Jensen are very unlikely to have had kids at St. George's, but they are *not* so unlikely to have *any connection at all* with St. George's. At the very least we should get Penny and Javi looking into connections between the victims and that school."

I nodded at the burgundy roof of my burgundy car for a while. "Yes," I said, and squinted up at the sky. "Yes, for the sake of completeness, tell Dominguez to focus on that. Leave O'Connor looking into Abdo."

I opened the car door and squinted at Dehan, who was still

sitting on the hood. "Truth, Dehan. This person is looking for a special kind of truth. Who looks for a special kind of truth?"

She shook her head and wagged a finger at me.

"No," she said. "Not this time, Stone. Shall I tell you what?"

As she walked around the hood and opened the passenger door, I said, "Tell me what."

"This case has appealed to that part of you that would have liked to be a philosopher. It has tickled your brain juice, and you want to plunge in and start asking all kinds of existential questions."

She climbed in and slammed the door. So I climbed in too and slammed mine, then turned the key in the ignition, and the big, old cat growled.

"But," she said, "this guy is not a brilliant philosopher who has found some sinister answer to the great questions of life. He is an asshole who gets his kicks torturing and killing people, and he uses philosophy as an excuse. This time, Sensei, you are barking up the wrong banyan tree."

I smiled as I turned onto West End Avenue. "I like that," I said, and then laughed. "Barking up the wrong banyan tree. That's funny. That's good."

She ignored me and called Dominguez, and told him to look for connections between the victims and St. George's Anglican School for Boys.

We cruised up through Manhattan, heading north in a general sort of way, allowing my mind to roam on a semiconscious level while enjoying all the rich variety and vitality of the heart and soul of New York. Afternoon was reaching a coppery middle age, and Manhattan's mind was turning to martinis, restaurants, and Broadway.

I thumped my walnut steering wheel gently a few times with the heel of my hand.

"Mathew Cavendish Jr. was tied to his furniture."

She shifted in her seat and turned to look at me. After a second, she slid her aviators up on her head like a medieval visor.

"Run that by me again, big guy." Before I could answer, she said, "He was on his back on a dining table."

"And?"

"Whoever killed him was *not* a Boy Scout or a sailor. He didn't know his knots. He made a mess of things and had . . ." She drew breath, sighed, and stared up at the canyons of steel as she tried to remember precisely. "He had his right leg tied to the leg of the table. His left leg, the rope wound around the other leg of the table and was tied with several knots to a Chesterfield armchair. There was another rope that went from his left wrist, under the table, around a third leg, and on to a Castilian oak coffee table with a heavy stone top, uhh . . ."

"It didn't stop there."

"No, this guy really didn't want him to get away. It went around the coffee table and went back to the Chesterfield. And the fourth rope went under the table, around the fourth table leg, to the coffee table, then around the leather, Chesterfield sofa, back to the chair, and around all four legs before being tied off."

"The knots themselves were fine, however, and it is noteworthy that the killer brought all that rope with him. I believe, Dehan, that the killer intended Cavendish to be aware, in his dying moments, that he was literally bound to his possessions."

"Huh . . ."

"The gas was on, causing asphyxia. The overall effect being of suffocation under all his wealth and possessions. It must have been a very unpleasant way to die."

"Detachment . . ."

"I am trying to imagine what his dying thoughts must have been."

"Why?"

I shook my head and sighed elaborately. "Those open questions, Dehan. Those open questions . . . !"

"Fine! What . . ." She hesitated.

"Because, Ritoo Glasshopper, I think the victim's dying thoughts might be important to the killer. These elaborate death scenes are not tableaus for the investigating detectives to ponder over. They are engineered, I believe, to make the condemned man or woman *think*."

"What makes you believe that?" she said, picking her words as though they were fruit on a bramble bush.

I answered with somewhat less care, "I am not sure yet, but I am sure. Quite sure."

We crossed the Harlem River, which is not really a river at all, and headed east toward the 43rd, still at a leisurely pace. As we were approaching the Bronx River I asked her, "Where is the drama, Dehan, in Judge Jeremiah Jones' death?"

"Seriously?"

"Play along. Describe his death for me, in detail, and as you do, try to identify where the drama lies."

"Okay . . ." She took a deep breath. "He was found in his chambers at 845 Walton Avenue. Not unlike Mathew Cavendish two years earlier, he had been tied to his desk. Though this time the binding was much less complicated. There was no other furniture involved. His head had been immobilized with two clamps so that he could not turn away. Then, a decorative sword was suspended from his chandelier by a rope that was attached, at the other end, to a heavy chair, and a candle was positioned under the rope so that the flame slowly burned through it. The candle, the rope, and the sword were all visible to him. A gag in his mouth made it impossible for him to scream."

"Good, now, question—" We crossed the Bronx River, and I came off for the Parkway. "Where was the drama in the way he was killed?"

She squinted at me. "I don't understand your question. I don't know what you're getting at."

"All of these murders are elaborately set up, right?"

"Right."

"So what part of this particular elaborate setup caused the drama?"

She shrugged and shook her head. I drew breath, and her cell rang.

"Yeah? Where . . . ? Okay, we're on our way." I made a question with my face and showed it to her. "They found the taxi. Outside the Spanish Seventh-day Adventist Church on Intervale Avenue, in Longwood."

"Good, call Joe, get him to come get the car. See what we can learn from it."

She was already doing it. So I relaxed and followed the nose of the Jag south along the Parkway, thinking about the dramatic part of Three Jay's death.

EIGHT

THE YELLOW FORD CROWN VICTORIA WAS OUTSIDE AN empty lot with a peeling, green plywood gate held closed by a rusty padlock that had been young when Methuselah had his bar mitzvah. Either side of the lot were redbrick walls painted with unimaginative graffiti, and beyond those were a range of tire shops, auto repair shops, and supermarkets that were not all that super and had window displays protected by metal mesh roller blinds. Parked in front of it was a patrol car with its lights flashing peacefully in the afternoon light.

I double-parked beside the cab with my hazards on, Dehan went to talk to the uniforms, and I pulled on some latex gloves and went to have a look at the cab. I peered through the windows and saw nothing remarkable. I tried the doors and found they were not locked. I poked my head in the driver's side and saw the keys still hanging from the ignition. Dehan leaned in the other side and spoke across the seats.

"They're not long here. They haven't touched the cab. They've spoken to a couple of the neighbors, but they are unforthcoming. That's what she said. She talks like you. You think maybe he's at the Sweaty Vest Café round the corner having coffee? Or you think maybe he left in a hurry?"

I popped the trunk and closed the door. "Maybe he was abducted by aliens."

I walked to the back, and Dehan joined me as I opened it up. There was the usual junk: a tool kit, triangles, hazard lights, and dirt. The dirt was dust, dry mud, bits of amorphous, unidentifiable "stuff."

"You got dry mud in your trunk, Dehan?"

"No, when I bury bodies I always use your car. Also I don't collect people from the airport on rainy days."

I grunted and nodded. Somewhere in the distance a siren howled. I slammed the trunk closed. Dehan, suppressing a grin, poked me on the chest.

"He's the guy."

"Did I ever say he wasn't?"

"You implied it, and you know it. You-did-not-think-he-was-the-guy! You-got-it-wrong, and I . . ." She gently stabbed her chest with her thumb. "*I* called it."

"Well, let's catch him and try him, shall we, before we start crowing."

She sneered and gloated and managed to make it look attractive. "*I* called it, and *you* got it wrong."

"You look very unattractive when you do that, Dehan," I lied.

"Yuh." She turned to watch the crime scene van pull up. Joe climbed out and came over while a couple of his boys started to pull on space suits and haul equipment out of the back of the van.

"We'll have a preliminary look here, then we'll take it back to the lab. Anything special you're looking for?"

I raised an eyebrow at Dehan. She hesitated a moment, and I told Joe, "Any evidence of an interest in religion or philosophy." I smiled at his look of surprise and went on. "You think I'm kidding. We are pretty sure he didn't transport any of his victims in the cab once they were dead, but evidence that he transported them when they were alive would be helpful. We're looking for a connection between the victims, and Dehan believes this taxi might be it . . ."

He pursed his lips and whistled. "That will be painstaking and slow, Carmen. We'll need to gather hair, tissue, or DNA, from the victims going back six years, and cross-reference it with what we find in the cab . . ."

I nodded. "Five years. We already know he had intimate contact with the first victim. We need to connect him with the other five. Also, any personal stuff you might find. I want to know who this guy is, where he comes from, and who he left behind."

He grimaced at Dehan. "Okay, we'll start by going over the cab to see what's there, then we'll get the filters out. I'll be in touch as soon as we have something—or as soon as we don't."

I thanked him and turned to Dehan. "You take the auto repair shop, I'll go talk to the tire shop. Maybe we can do better than your erudite sergeant."

"Gotcha."

The tire shop was maybe fifty feet away, and there was a big guy with dreadlocks leaning on the doorjamb eating an apple and watching us. He kept watching and chewing as I approached. I showed him my badge and made a civil face.

"Detective John Stone, NYPD. Did you happen to see who left that cab there?"

He made no expression, but his eyes gave me a once-over, and he shook his head. His voice was deep. "I already told your uniform." He bit into his apple again.

"How long have you been standing there?"

He shrugged, first with his eyebrows, then with his shoulders. He took another bite, and he was down to the core.

"This your shop?"

Something shifted in his eyes, which went from insolent to dangerous. "Uh-huh."

I took a step back and turned and pointed at the yellow cab. "I think that cab was in your workshop. Those tires look new to me. Hey! Joe!"

Joe turned to look at me. "What?"

"Those tires, they look new to you?"

I saw his eyes flick up at the sign, and he smiled. "They could be. It's possible."

"See? Now I have probable cause. I think that you have interfered with evidence and aided and abetted a suspect in his escape. I suspect that your workshop was used to destroy evidence. So I am going to have to shut the place down while the crime scene boys . . ."

"Okay! Okay! Okay!" He turned and threw the apple core at a trash can and scored a hit. "Guy parked his car there. So what?"

"What did he look like?"

"Shit, man, how the hell should I know? I heard the car stop. He was in a hurry. He got in another car, and he was gone."

"Come on! Tall, short, fat, thin, black, white, Chinese . . ."

"Brother."

"What?"

His big face went hard, like he really wanted to hit me. "He was a *brother*!"

"The car he got into, was it waiting for him, or did it just show up?"

"I don't know. I didn't notice."

"What kind of car was it?" He opened his mouth, and by his face I knew what he was going to say. I didn't waste time. I turned and called to Joe. "Hey! Joe!" He turned to look at me. I said, "We're going to need to do this whole workshop. We'll need to impound the cars. You got the team . . . ?"

He puffed out his cheeks. "I could put a couple of guys on it . . . Maybe start next week . . ."

Dreadlocks growled. "Just wait a minute, will ya?"

I looked back at him. "Are you sure we understand each other? Because giving false evidence is just about as serious as withholding evidence. Either way I shut your damned workshop and impound all the damned cars for the next three weeks—if you're lucky."

"You made your point, cop. It was an old BMW, Three Series, 'bout 2005. Either black or dark blue. It was waiting just 'cross the road. Dude in the cab rolled up in a hurry, jumped out, got in the bimmer, and took off high speed."

"Which way did he go?"

He spat slowly and elaborately at his feet. "South."

"What about the driver?"

"What about him?"

"What did he look like?"

"I didn't see no driver. Now, if you will excuse me, Mr. Pig Officer, I done about all the helping I can do. I don't know no more."

He turned and swaggered inside, swinging his shoulders in an exaggerated way. I turned and made my way across the road to join Dehan, who was stepping into the barbershop on the far side. It was empty but for the barber, a big, sallow guy in his fifties who regarded us with distaste as he swept the floor.

"You scared off all my customers."

Dehan answered. "What were they scared of?"

He snorted with a small amount of humor, and I got the feeling if we didn't push him, he might be helpful. His big plate glass window offered a panoramic view of the yellow taxi and the space where the BMW had been parked. I jerked my head at it.

"It's a good view."

"You don't need to fence with me, Detective. I am a law-abiding citizen, like my father and my grandfather and my great-grandfather before me." He put away his dustpan and broom and eyed me with irony cultivated over generations of living with raw reality. "You don't reach these heights in the barbering industry by getting on the wrong side of the Bronx police force. What do you want?"

Dehan told him. "We're looking for the man who was driving that taxi. Did you see him arrive?"

He nodded. "I saw him arrive. It was maybe half an hour ago, a little more. He came down the road like a thing possessed. Screeched to a halt and almost fell getting out of his taxi . . ."

I interrupted. "How long before that had the BMW arrived?"

"About ten minutes before. Not much more than that." He shrugged. "They are things that happen every day in this neighborhood. You don't really notice them unless something happens."

Dehan asked, "So what did happen?"

"Like I said." He gestured with his open hand at the window. "The BMW pulled up. Nothing happened, nobody got out, nobody got in. Like I said, normal. Then ten minutes later the taxi come tearing down the road like it had all the bats out of hell on its tail. He screams to a halt, half falls out of the door, and runs to the BMW. He gets in . . ."

"Back or front?"

"Um . . ." He stared up at the ceiling. "Back. Then the BMW took off at a respectable speed. Nothing that would make the cops stop them." He gave us a look that had more than a hint of contempt in it. "The cops in the Bronx don't stop BMW Three Series with dangerous black drivers in them unless they really have to. The gangs are privileged. You know what privilege is, Detectives?" We didn't answer, but he didn't expect us to. He went right on. "Privilege comes from the Latin, *privus legis,* private law. The gangs around here enjoy a law which is all their own, and the cops recognize their jurisdiction."

I shook my head. "I assure you that is not the case, Mr. . . ."

I paused. He raised an eyebrow at me.

"Mr. Blinderman, and you can assure me of whatever you like. I am more inclined to trust my eyes than my ears." He tapped his right ear. "Your ears catch what people say, but your eyes tell you what people do."

Dehan sighed. There wasn't a lot you could answer to a statement that was patently true. "Did you recognize any of them? The driver or the guy from the taxi?"

He nodded. "Yes, I recognized them. They are Sudanese. They belong to a gang. It's not like one of those Latino gangs or the Angels, they have names like the Bloods, Satan's Soldiers . . ." He paused to laugh a laugh that had matured over years in nicotine and wine. "This gang has no name. They have seen too much reality, too much slaughter and rape and massacre to play with names. They are united by a belief in Allah as the one God and Mohamed as his prophet, and their own intrinsic superiority over all other humans. They are the elect, God's favored heroes, who will go direct to paradise and enjoy *at least* eighty thousand servants and seventy-two *houri* to pleasure them."

"Are you telling us they are jihadists?"

"I'm not telling you that. I have no idea if they are terrorists or not. But I know they have weapons and they have no shortage of money. I know they sell drugs, and I know that the other gangs around here are afraid of them. They are not 'taking over' . . ." He made the sign with his fingers. "Or anything like that. They keep a low profile, they do their thing, and nobody bothers them." He held up both hands. "But please, remember, I am just the neighborhood barber. I live upstairs and I rarely leave my premises. I am telling you what my customers tell me while I am cutting their hair."

I said, "Your customers ever mention any names or addresses?"

He snorted his ironic laugh again. "This one, the one in the cab, his name is Abdo. I don't know his surname, but he comes in here for a haircut sometimes. He calls me a *kalb yahudiun,* a Jewish dog. The two boys in the front looked like his friends Kamal and Mustafa. They usually hang out together. It looks as though he got into some trouble and called on them to get him out."

"What else do they tell you about Abdo and his pals?" He looked at me for a long time. His face said he was a strong, brave man who obeyed his conscience. It also told me that he knew he was risking his own life, and maybe that of his family, by talking to me for so long.

"They say he likes women, but he likes to hurt them. The . . . the girls around here won't go with him anymore unless they have no choice. I have seen a few of his girls after he has finished with them. He beats them, accuses them of being whores, cuts them, and tells them they will burn in hell for eternity."

"What about their pimps? Most pimps don't like their property to get damaged."

He spread his hands. "I don't know any details. Like I said, I am just a barber. I heard there was some trouble about a year ago. A couple of pimps left town and showed up eventually on the beach on Long Island, a little bloated and blue. Word was Abdo and his friends were told to cool down, and a young guy called Jamal was offered as a scapegoat. After that things cooled down a bit."

"So Abdo no longer preys on the local sex workers?"

"That's what I hear." We were silent for a while, then Blinderman said suddenly, "I won't swear to any of this in court, you understand that?"

I nodded. "Sure."

"Not until the cops can offer us some kind of protection against these animals. This . . ." He pointed at the window, and suddenly his face was twisted with bitterness and hate. "This is *unspeakable*. This *trash* has more protection from the law than we have. They prey on us, they exploit us, they brutalize us, and you!" He waved his hand at us. "*You!* You stand by and watch it happen and talk about *their* rights!"

Dehan glanced at me, then asked, "They take protection money from you?"

"Of course they do! You know they do . . ."

I turned toward the door and took hold of the handle. I drew breath to speak but didn't know what to say. In the end I just said, "I'm sorry."

He shook his head and dismissed us with a shake of his hand, and we stepped out into the failing afternoon.

NINE

WE CRUISED DOWN INTERVALE TILL WE CAME TO THE intersection with Longwood. Then we crossed under the Bruckner Expressway and turned left toward Lafayette. We were going slow, and Dehan was sitting in the back. It didn't take long to see what we were looking for.

She was standing on the corner of Lafayette and Tiffany, in the shelter of the trees in the Corpus Christi gardens. It wasn't dusk yet, but the copper light of late afternoon was turning grainy, and she was almost lost among the dappled shadows. I pulled over and leaned out. My car is right-hand drive, so I was on the sidewalk side and called to her.

"Hey, sweetheart, can you give me directions?"

Wherever she was from, it wasn't Hollywood. She had peroxide-blond hair and the sallow skin of a heroin addict, a low-cut blouse over unnaturally large breasts, and jeans so tight you could almost hear her legs squeak when she walked. On her feet she had glittering, crimson high heels. She forced a smile on her scarlet lips and approached without enthusiasm.

"Where you are wanting to go?"

I winked at her. "Me and my friend"—I jerked my head

toward the back of the car—"we wanted to have a party, so we thought it would be nice to bring along a friend."

She peered in the back, and Dehan gave her a small wave.

"Special is two hundred bucks . . ." She glanced over the Jag and said, "Special is three hundred bucks. We go your place?"

"In Manhattan."

"Five hundred bucks, for the risk. Lots of crazy people."

"Oh, we just want to have a nice time, some champagne, watch some movies, smoke some weed . . . You know what I'm saying?"

"Okay, two fifty now, two fifty when finish."

I laughed. "I'll tell you what, I'll double it if you'll be nice and smile." I didn't wait for an answer and leaned back. "You got the cash, honey?"

Dehan was counting it out in the back seat. "Got it right here, sweetheart." She leaned over and opened the door. "C'mon, get in. Let me get a look at you. What's your name?"

"Irena."

Irena's eyes had caught sight of the cash, and her pupils had dilated to the size of her irises. She pulled the door fully open and climbed in. I pulled away and headed for the expressway. In the mirror I saw Dehan hold up the two hundred and fifty bucks.

"This is yours, Irena, to do whatever you want with it. But there is a condition attached to it."

Irena was looking worried. "What condition? You say we go party, champagne . . ."

I gave a small laugh. "Here's the thing, Irena: I lied. We are cops. I am Detective John Stone, and this is Detective Dehan."

Dehan took over. "Now, if I were doing my job right, at this moment I would arrest you and hand you over to Vice, and my guess is you would do serious time, and they would force you to get clean. Am I right, Stone?"

"You're not wrong. And if she tries anything, slap the cuffs on her and sit on her head. Or shoot her."

I heard her laugh. "My partner, he's a bit tough. Me? I prefer dialogue. I think most things can be worked out by talking to people. For example, we are not Vice. So we actually have no interest in your problem with drugs, who sells it to you, where he gets it from, all that. But we *are* interested in a client you might have had, or some of your friends might have had. So, you talk to us, you take home your money, we get our guy, win-win, right?"

Her eyes were wild. The way they were darting around you'd swear there were twenty people in the back of the Jag and she was trying to keep tabs on all of them at the same time.

"Who is guy? Why you ask me? Why not ask another?"

I smiled at the mirror. "Because it's your lucky day, Irena. God has chosen you for his sunbeam."

"Where we going?"

Dehan placed a hand on her shoulder. "We're just going to drive around for a while and talk. Then we'll leave you back where we found you, okay?"

We were up on the freeway, headed toward the 43rd. The dusk was closing in, and the streetlamps and headlamps were starting to come on. She was completely silent five long seconds with the flowing lights pulsing over her face in a slow rhythm. Then the explosion came. Dehan was ready for her, and as Irena reached, screaming, for the door, she lunged, slipped her arm around her neck, and pulled her back.

I kept the car steady, glancing in the mirror at Irena's goggling face and thrashing arms and legs. One of her breasts popped out of her blouse, and her bag fell to the floor as she clawed at Dehan's forearm. I reached back with my left hand and grabbed it. The least dangerous thing it could contain was pepper spray. Dirty needles was the worst.

One of her scarlet high heels fell off, and she planted her foot against the back of my seat. She was making a horrible gargling noise. Dehan's face was lost behind her mass of blond hair, but I saw her loop one of her long, slim legs over Irena's and pull it down. Irena went still, and after a moment I heard Dehan growl in her ear, "You want the two hundred and fifty bucks or not, you crazy . . ."

She trailed off and didn't utter the final word. Three long seconds passed, and finally Irena nodded. I held up her bag for her to see and said, "I haven't looked inside, but I figure you have things here you'll need when you leave, so my advice is, be smart and leave with a smile, two hundred and fifty bucks, and your purse. Plus the goodwill of the New York Police Department. We have a deal?"

There was a muffled croak that might have been a "yes."

Dehan let her go. She pulled away and flounced into the corner of the back seat.

"Freaks!"

I exchanged a smile with Dehan in the mirror and said, "You ready to talk?"

"I not no grass. I not going to grass nobody up."

"That's fine. We are looking for a man who maybe hurts girls."

There was a moment of stillness. Outside, the dusk was quickening toward evening. The westbound headlamps were becoming a steady river of light. Irena's face faded in and out of darkness in my mirror.

"Hurts girls?"

Dehan answered her. "Yes, we think so. We think he hates women, he pays them and then hurts them. Do you know anybody like that?"

"I know couple, yes. And for this I get money?"

"Yes."

"And my purse?"

"Yes. Who are the men you know like this, Irena?"

"There was Greg, it make two years back now. He was like to take cocaine and then ride girl hard and whip her. So girls is okay like this. But Greg take too much coca and one day hurt girl real bad, and Sly, is her boy, he go find Greg and . . ."

"And what?"

"He cut his throat, put him in river."

Dehan glanced at me and sighed. We were approaching the Bronx River Parkway interchange. Dehan was saying, "Yeah, that's great, Irena, but the guy we are looking for is alive. He is maybe hurting girls right now. Is there anyone the girls talk about?"

"Maybe Abbo."

"Abbo?"

"He is black boy, not from America. He is from Africa. He like to hurt girls too. He like it too much. Every week, two, three times, him and his friends. Sometimes more. He pay money, sometimes he don't pay, not money."

I said, "What do you mean? He pays, but not money? He pays with something else?"

"Yah."

"Like what?"

"Sometimes maybe gun, or he make a favor."

"What kind of favor, Irena?"

I peeled off onto Bruckner Boulevard and began to slow. I was watching her face in the mirror, suddenly plunged into shadow by the overpass, then flooded by the lights of Metcalf Avenue. She looked startled and scared, and her mascara and her lipstick were smudged.

"Girls say he kill people. You need somebody dead, he kill. He fix problems for people. I don't like talk about him."

Dehan put a hand on her shoulder. "Did you ever go with him?"

"Couple times only, in party with other girls."

She started to cry, big, ugly sobs. We were passing Fteley Avenue, and for a moment I thought about pulling her in as a material witness. But I dismissed it. Her evidence was practically all hearsay, and if she had any value, it was where she was. I kept going to Rosedale and switched back onto the Boulevard, going west.

Dehan was asking, "What does he look like, Irena?"

She spoke through sobs. "Tall, thin, strong. Cruel face . . ." She waved her hands in front of her face. "Cruel eyes and mouth. After party, lots of coca, and drink, he tell us, 'Go now, go home!' but he make Mina stay."

"Mina?"

"Mina friend from Ukraine."

"He made her stay with him?"

She nodded; her mouth twisted and bunched, her cheeks shiny with tears. "He make her stay and she never come back. I ask Sly . . ."

"Sly is your boy?"

"All girls in Tiffany, Barretto, Manida . . ."

"Okay, I get it, so you spoke to him . . ."

She nodded. "And he tell me, 'Forget, never again ask, she is gone.' I tell him, 'Fuck you! Where is she?' and he beat me hard. I can't walk for week. I want go home to Ukraine."

She folded forward, her elbows tucked into her belly and her face sobbing into her hands. I caught Dehan's eye in the mirror. She knew why I had passed by Fteley, and her expression said she wasn't convinced my decision was right. My expression must have told her the same thing.

She stroked Irena's back for a moment, then asked her.

"Could you identify him for us?"

She sat up straight like she'd been given an electric shock. "No!"

"Okay, take it easy. Nobody is going to force you to do anything you don't want to do."

I asked into the mirror, "Do you know where he is now?"

"Hiding."

"Yeah, we know that. Do you know where?"

An almost imperceptible nod. Then, "What happen to him if you catch?"

Dehan answered. "The best thing that will happen to that son of a bitch is that he will go to prison for the rest of his life. But with luck, he'll try to resist arrest."

I sighed and thanked whatever gods look after cops that the chief had not been listening in.

"There is warehouse on Story Avenue, at end, by river. Abbo is friend of owner. Many time owner give him place to hide if there is trouble."

Dehan asked, "Have you been there?"

"Once, with other girls. Is office of warehouse. There is bathroom, sofa. He can stay at there and his friends bring him food, drink, girls, anything he needs."

I skipped the feed onto the expressway and kept going until I reached Bronx River Avenue. As I turned left into it, I said to Irena, "Point it out to me."

I heard a small gasp. In the mirror I saw her hand over her mouth and her eyes searching the windows. Then she pointed. "This one. Is this one here."

There was no sign from the outside that anyone was in the building. There were few windows, and they were small, and no light leaked out from them. There was a big yard fenced off with corrugated sheets of steel. I could see there were big lamps to floodlight the place, but they were dark too. We cruised by and continued along Story.

Story Avenue is a mile and a quarter long and runs all the way from the river to White Plains Road. It's had a face-lift here and there, but the river end is still what you might call "old Bronx." And about halfway along, on the left, is Fteley Avenue, and the station house of the 43rd Precinct. That was where we went.

When we got there Irena started doing her hysterics again, and Dehan got the worst of it. In the end a couple of uniforms came running out and helped drag her from the car and put her in protective custody. We opened her bag and found a couple of grams of coke, along with the kind of makeup you'd use if you wanted to give somebody nightmares. We bagged it and put it into evidence and went up to talk to the chief. But first we spoke to O'Connor, who had gathered what she could on Abdo Deng.

"He's on our watch list, and he is also on the bureau's watch list as having possible terrorist connections. He's been pulled in for questioning several times here and at the Forty-First in relation to several cases of violence: knife fights, beatings, and a couple of homicides, as well as prostitution, drugs, and firearms. Nothing has ever stuck. Here is a full, written report, Detective."

I ignored her smile and the batting of her eyelashes, and Dehan and I climbed the stairs.

The chief smiled benignly at us as we entered.

"Ah, the dynamic duo. How are things progressing? You have news . . ." It wasn't a question, but I nodded as we sat, and he asked, "How are O'Connor and Dominguez working out?"

"They are just fine, sir. Sir, let me come straight to the point. We need a stakeout, and we need it twenty-four hours ago. And we need it round the clock."

He sank back in his chair and raised his eyebrows about as high as he could raise them. He placed his fingertips carefully on the edge of the desk and said, "Ah . . ."

Dehan didn't let him answer. "We have the guy, sir."

He turned to her, and his eyebrows clawed another eighth of an inch from his brow.

"You have? So soon?"

"Detective Dehan and I are not absolutely at one on that point, sir, but we have a candidate who it seems very likely is guilty of multiple murders, gun trafficking, drug trafficking, and probably has terrorist connections too . . ."

He grinned without humor. "I give you one case, you solve another?"

Dehan leaned forward. "No, sir. He is a suspect in the Jensen case, but as we looked into him, this whole other aspect opened up. He works as a taxicab driver . . ."

"He is a master criminal and terrorist, and he moonlights as a cab driver?"

Dehan stood up, went up and down on her toes a couple of times, and sat down again.

"No, sir. It is complex, but it seems that cab driving is some kind of a cover. The fact is that when we called his boss and gave him a message to tell Abdo Deng . . ."

"Abdo Deng . . ."

"Yes, sir. When we told him to ask him to come in and talk to us, he ran. We have testimony from two witnesses that he has a record of violence against women, and that he is involved in sadistic acts against prostitutes, that he is a hit man for local crime bosses, and that he is involved in gun running and drugs. We know where he is, and we know that he has people bringing him food, drink, and possibly girls."

"Good Lord!"

I said, "He is just down the road, at the end of Story Avenue."

"What is your opinion, John? You said you differ from Carmen."

"Not in essence, sir. I am just not ready to commit yet. There is a very good chance he is our man. There is no doubt in my mind, from what I have seen and heard, that he is guilty of murder and torture. I am just not one hundred percent sure he killed these six other people. But he is a very dangerous man, and we need to take him off the streets."

"What do you want?"

"I want a twenty-four-hour watch, and the minute we are sure he's there, I want to storm the place and take him."

TEN

He granted my wish and put two teams on rotating twelve-hour shifts. After that, we made our way downstairs, I handed Dehan the key to the car, and while she went to pull it out of the lot, I went to the detectives' room to get my laptop. I was surprised to see Dominguez still sitting at my desk. He looked up and smiled as I approached.

"Good evening, Detective. I was hoping to catch you before you left, you've been rushed off your feet since you arrived."

"What is it?"

"You asked me to look into Cavendish and any clubs or religious groups he might have belonged to."

"I did."

"He has never belonged to any religious groups as such, and in fact he has given speeches at the Ingersoll Institute and published a few articles in *The Free Thinker* and the *Philosopher's Monthly*, strongly denouncing religion as a pernicious influence on society."

"Has he?" I sat.

"Yes, he seemed pretty passionate about it, and vocal. But he did attend a series of courses at the Bronx Vihara on . . ." He leafed through his papers. ". . . in fall and winter of 2015, in

Buddhist psychology, dhamma, and karma—or as it's spelt here, kamma. I looked it up. Apparently it's the Pali spelling as opposed to the Sanskrit spelling. It seems Buddhism was originally taught in Pali, not Sanskrit. So he seems to have been very interested in Buddhism."

I sank back in my chair and remained blank for a couple of minutes, thinking about what he had just told me. I frowned at him. "Have you written out a report?"

"Sure, it's here. That and the other stuff I've managed to find. I'm afraid it's not a lot."

He handed it to me, and I sat leafing through the few pages for a while. I spoke, nodding at the file and staring at the pages.

"It's good. Good work. Tomorrow I want you back sifting through the other victims' backgrounds."

"Sure thing, Detective."

I thanked him and went out to where Dehan was waiting, leaning against the Jag in a pool of lamplight. I stood across from her and opened the passenger door, then paused.

"Aside from the Chinese government and the Chinese Red Army, why would anyone want to kill a Buddhist?"

She looked vaguely surprised. "I have no idea, Stone."

She climbed in, and I climbed in beside her. "Islam's big beef has always been with what they call 'the people of the book,' Jews and Christians. Initially the Jews because Judaism was the dominant religion in that area at that time, but gradually as Christianity rose into ascendancy, it became their archenemy."

She was backing out of the lot, peering over her shoulder and glancing at me occasionally to show she was listening. As she pulled onto Story Avenue she said, "So?"

"Like I said, apart from the Chinese government, I can't think of anybody, or any body, that would want to go around killing Buddhists, and as far as I am aware, Islam has not declared a jihad against Buddhism."

"There was the case of the Bamyan Buddhas in Afghanistan that were destroyed by the Taliban."

I grunted. "It was a stupid, ignorant thing to do, but it wasn't exactly a declaration of jihad."

"Why this, anyway, Stone?" She spun the wheel and turned onto White Plains. "The guy is probably a Muslim, and two of the victims had an interest in Buddhism; that is hardly a jihad against Buddha."

"You're forgetting Jensen; he was a practicing Buddhist, remember?"

She was quiet for a while, cruising north on White Plains, then shrugged and shook her head.

"It feels like a coincidence because the three victims we have looked into so far have had some connection with Buddhism. I don't know for a fact, because I haven't looked into it, but my guess is Buddhism is the fastest-growing religion right now." She glanced at me. "It's sexy to be a Buddhist, right? They care, they talk about compassion, and they don't start wars. And above all, it's big in Hollywood: Keanu Reeves, Brad Pitt, Angelina Jolie, lots of others. These days, everywhere you look there's a guy with real short hair and sandals baking his own brown bread." After a pause she added, "Being real nice to his cat."

We laughed, and I told her maybe she was right.

But later, at home, while the Bolognese was simmering, I went online and said, "Actually, you're wrong."

She frowned at me from the kitchen where she was filling a pot with water.

"What about?"

I made a long "hmmm" sound. "It's one of those statistical things where the facts suggest one thing, but the truth is otherwise."

"This again?"

She put salt in the water and put it on to boil.

"Technically, the fastest-growing religion in the world is Islam, but that is because of three dynamics, two of which are peculiar to Islam. One, Muslim families tend to have more kids; two, in recent decades there has been an aggressive expansion of Islam and a tendency to fundamentalism, so people who might not otherwise be Muslim are counted as Muslim. And third, there has been a very large amount of emigration from the Middle East to Europe and the States, which has contributed to the *geographical* spread of Islam, if not the cultural spread."

She was still frowning, but now she was leaning on the breakfast bar with her forearms. She said, "Right . . ."

"Buddhism, on the other hand, is also growing fast, but in a different way. With Buddhism it is the ideas that are spreading. Buddhism is increasingly seen as a philosophy rather than a religion. It is not a religion that has ever sought converts, so in terms of card-carrying members, it lags behind Christianity and Islam, but in terms of people who espouse Buddhist ideas, we would probably get a different result."

"Where are you going with this, Stone?"

I put my laptop on the coffee table and stood. "Georgina Cheng, eminent chemist and a leading light in antiviral research, the fifth victim of our killer, rose to notoriety because of several interviews she gave in defense of vivisection."

"Was found with her limbs amputated . . ."

"And traces of curare were found in her blood, suggesting she was conscious when the amputations took place."

"Beyond horrific, but what about her?"

"Dominguez traced her family back to Hong Kong, and both her parents were Buddhists. She was brought up a Buddhist, though she did not practice." She sighed loudly. I went on, "However you want to explain it, Dehan, that is four out of six, sixty-six percent. It is a significant percentage, and we haven't looked at the others yet." Over her shoulder I saw the pot steaming. "The water is boiling."

She turned and started dumping spaghetti into the pot.

"Even if it is statistically significant, Stone. How? In what way is it significant? If Abdo Deng is killing people on some private jihad against Buddhism, there must be millions of people he could target. Why these? They're not actively promoting

Buddhism. In fact, Jensen was the only real, practicing Buddhist among them."

"Just because we can't see it doesn't mean it isn't there. The fact is that every one of them so far has had some connection with Buddhism."

She picked up a long stick of spaghetti that had fallen from the pack and waved it at me. "Well I am pretty sure your run of Buddhists has come to an end and it is no more than a statistical fluke. Saul Arender was a dyed-in-the-wool Jew, and Judge Jeremiah Jones, Three Jay, was a dyed-in-the-wool American evangelist. You will not find any kind of Buddhist connections there."

"You want to bet?"

"Against you? No thanks. You cheat."

"Ha!" I made my way to the kitchen to collect the cutlery for the table. "The cry of vanquished women everywhere. 'You cheat!'"

"Jerk!"

THE CALL CAME at four a.m. I was expecting it, so I was half awake anyway. I fumbled for my cell and sat up.

"Yeah, Stone."

"Detective, this is Sergeant Kauffmann. Me and Merino are watching the warehouse on Story."

"Yeah, something's happened?"

"Yeah, we have instructions to call you direct. Two guys arrived in an old Three Series dark BMW and let themselves in. About . . . two minutes ago."

"Were they carrying anything?"

"We don't know. They went inside with the car, into the yard."

"Okay, we'll be there in twenty minutes. Keep me posted."

Dehan was already swinging out of bed headed for the bathroom. I followed her, talking, dialing the chief. "Looks like Mustafa and Kamal have arrived at the warehouse . . . Yeah, good morning, sir, it looks like Mustafa and Kamal have arrived at the warehouse. They let themselves in about two minutes ago, took the car inside too."

"Any weapons on view? Any indication of drugs . . . ?"

"Only the fact that the car, at . . ." I checked. "Five minutes to four in the morning drove into a warehouse where we have witness testimony that Abdo Deng is hiding out."

A heavy sigh. "All right, we have a SWAT team on standby. I'll see you there in twenty minutes."

"We're on our way."

Half an hour later we were standing with the inspector outside the big, rusty-red warehouse at the end of Story Avenue. There was a predawn chill in the air, and the limpid light from the streetlamps gave the broad roads a depressing gloom.

We were thirty or forty yards from the big gates that gave onto the yard and the door that led to the offices and the warehouse proper. There was no indication on the outside of what kind of goods they stored or shipped. There was just a board over the door with blue writing that said, *Consolidated International Shipping and Storage Co.*

There were two patrol cars at the corner, blocking off Bronx River Avenue, ten or fifteen yards from the warehouse gate. Another two stood across Story, about fifteen feet from where we stood at the inspector's car. And across the road from the gate, on the far side of the road, were a big, chunky SWAT van and an armored vehicle. They had their instructions, and they knew what they were doing.

Dehan and I had our instructions too: put on your body armor, wait till SWAT have done their stuff. Then, when you're not in the way, go in and detect. It was a routine I was familiar with and comfortable with. If I had wanted to be a warrior, I'd have joined the army. But I could see that Dehan was not so comfortable. There was a gleam in her eye when she looked over at the trucks that said she wanted to be there, charging, clearing one room after another until she found Abdo.

A loud, flat detonation echoed across the predawn street, and then we were running toward the SWAT van, and the SWAT team was running toward the smoldering gate in the shelter of the armored vehicle. The gate crumpled and tore from its hinges as the Mega plowed over it and the team took up positions on either side. There were a couple of shouts from inside and a couple of short bursts of automatic fire. The team leader looked back and held up his hand for us to wait. Then there were instructions being shouted, echoing flat and surreal in the empty, quiet street.

A voice roared, *"NYPD! Lay down your weapons and put up your hands!"*

A pause, and the same voice: *"Hands where I can see them! Hands where I can see them!"*

And then the insane crackling, like a box of firecrackers had caught fire. Shouts, inarticulate and meaningless at this distance. I heard Dehan swear, and suddenly she was racing across the street toward the gate. I bellowed at her, *"Dehan! Come back here!"*

I went after her at a furious sprint. Bullets whined and sung as they ricocheted off the armored car. One spat up a column of dust a foot from where Dehan had thrown herself flat against the wall beside the gate. I did the same, placing myself between her and the opening.

"Dehan! You will withdraw to a safe distance and await the instructions of the SWAT team leader!"

A hail of fire tore through the fence and made me duck away. As I did so Dehan turned and ran three steps to the door to the offices. A bellowed order told her to stand clear. That door was being covered from the outside to nab the bad guys if they tried to escape that way. Dehan blew out the lock, kicked the door in, and went in. I went after her. As I tore in after her, she turned and glared at me and put her finger to her lips.

I glared back, pointed to the door, and mouthed, *Go back!*

She ignored me and continued into the office area. There was a short passage with a large warehouse door at the end. To either side there were offices painted beige, and at the end was a staircase which climbed to an upper floor. I knew what she was going to do and beat her to it. I ran, flattened myself against the wall, and stared up into the stairwell with my gun trained on the banisters and the upper landing. There was no one there, and Dehan ran lightly up the first flight. There she covered the landing, and I ran up the next flight. She followed, and we found ourselves in a broad space with a desk, a round coffee table, and some chairs. To the left of that was an office door, and opposite were the toilets. There were no people, but we could hear muffled gunfire and shouts.

I tapped Dehan on the shoulder, scowled, shook my head, and mouthed, *No!*

She nodded briefly and ran across the landing to crouch beside the office door. I swore violently and silently and followed her. As I crouched at the other side of the door, she put her fingers to her lips and carefully tried the handle. The door eased open.

I mouthed, *Are you insane?*

She frowned slightly, nodded once, lay on her belly, and eased the door a little farther.

Just about the only thing in my mind was the image of her head and back being peppered with gunfire. That wasn't an option, so I stood, stepped in front of her, pushed the door open, and went down on one knee, so she was covered.

It was a large room, about the size of a small apartment, with a mezzanine floor. There was a desk on the far right, on the upper level, with an arrangement of white leather armchairs and sofas. On the lower level there was a copper fireplace in the middle of the floor, thick, white bearskin rugs, more overstuffed leather furniture, and a large, red vinyl bar. There were no people—not there in the room.

What people there were, were out on a terrace overlooking the loading yard. There were five of them. I recognized Abdo in the middle, but the others were indistinct. They all had assault rifles, and they were all shooting down at the SWAT team.

Dehan got to her feet and strode across the room. Alarm turned to terror as she did so. There was no time to stop her, and even if there had been I knew it was not possible. So I ran. She saw me and laughed and ran too. Between us we burst onto the terrace, bellowing at the top of our voices, "*Freeze! Drop your weapons! NYPD!*"

They didn't. We knew they wouldn't, and we were ready for them. There was a moment of confusion where they turned to face us. Abdo shouted something, and he and Kamal and another turned back to answer the shots coming from below. But a guy I didn't know lined me up, and Mustafa trained his weapon straight at Dehan. I let my legs go and dropped. On the way down I put nine slugs into Mustafa's chest, while all around me the air sang and popped and powdered concrete spattered my face.

I hit the ground hard and saw the guy who'd been shooting at me slide down the parapet, leaving a thick red line behind him. Kamal was turning, and I shot instinctively at twelve feet. Both rounds punched through his heart. Dehan was efficient. She had barely moved her stance. She double tapped the guy beside Abdo, and Abdo held up both hands and stepped toward her, to avoid the fire from below. He still had his weapon in his hand, and I saw it twitch. Dehan snarled, "On your knees!" and put a slug through his right thigh. He screamed, tottered, and fell. I stepped over and kicked his weapon away. I bellowed, "*NYPD! Clear! All clear!*" Then I knelt beside him and frisked him thoroughly for more weapons. He had a Sig Sauer P320 Legion, a bowie in his boot, and a slim switchblade in his jacket.

Abdo was weeping, clutching at his leg. When he spoke, through wet, blubbering lips, his voice was surprisingly deep, which was a bit bizarre and surreal, because he was crying like a child.

"She shot me!" he said. "I surrender and she shoot me. I was giving up my weapon and she shoot me . . ."

Dehan came up real close and lowered her head next to his. I could hear the tramp of running boots downstairs. Her voice was barely a hiss. "You like hurting women, you son of a bitch? Thank your god SWAT were here. If we'd been alone, it wouldn't have been your leg I shot."

She stood and looked me straight in the eye.

"I'm sorry, Stone. I know you didn't appreciate that. They had SWAT pinned down, and a rearguard action was the only way. Team leader was taking too long to give the order." She shrugged. "Judgment call."

I shook my head. "You're out of your mind, but I'll back you up. You know I will."

ELEVEN

THE SWAT TEAM LEADER WAS NOT HAPPY, AND NEITHER was the inspector. He had serious and severe words with Dehan, and with me, and the words "reckless" and "negligent" were tossed around a little too freely. But Dehan made her case, and I backed her up.

"Chief, the team were under unexpectedly heavy fire from an elevated position. They were pinned down, and the team leader was taking too long to make a decision which was obvious and critical. Lives were at risk, and it was becoming merely a question of time before somebody got shot.

"I am well trained in firearms, sir, and I have done courses in urban combat. I knew that unless we started a rearguard action to draw their fire, one of the SWAT team was going to get shot. I had to act, and I had to act quickly and decisively. Detective Stone and I were able to coordinate a rearguard attack with minimum risk to ourselves or anybody else, while avoiding injury to the SWAT team."

I said, "It's true, sir."

He stood blinking at her for a long time. Then he blinked at me. In the end all he could say was, "Your reports, on my desk by this afternoon. I *will* compare and contrast them with the SWAT team's reports."

"Yes, sir."

I echoed that and asked, "How soon can we talk to Abdo?"

"He is on his way to the hospital now. We'll have to wait for the doctor's report."

The head of the SWAT team stepped out onto the terrace and gave Dehan a look that said he was unimpressed.

"I don't like what you did, Detective Dehan. It was my operation, and I told you to stay put." He turned to me. "But I have to say, the warehouse was a good call. Downstairs there is a whole lot of junk, but among the junk there is at least half a ton of cocaine, and another half ton easy of heroin. And we only just got started. God alone knows what else we are going to find there."

She stepped up to him and slapped him on the shoulder. "Detective Stone tends to make good calls. But it wasn't the only good call we made this morning. If I hadn't taken the office, you would have been screwed and lost men. It takes a big man to recognize he's wrong. Be a big man, pal." She turned to the chief. "We're going to try and talk to our witness, sir. We'll have our reports on your desk this afternoon."

They watched us leave without saying anything.

We didn't say anything to each other until we had climbed in the car and I had fired up the engine. Then we sat in silence a moment longer while I steadied my heartbeat and my breathing.

"Are you mad at me?"

"That depends on whom you are talking to. Detective John Stone or plain old John Stone." Her face, slightly luminous in the dawn light, turned to look at me and waited. "As a cop, as the head of our team, as the lead in this investigation, I admire what you did and I think you made the right call, even if there was a touch of insubordination involved. It was the right call."

"Thank you."

"As your husband, and the father of our future children, as plain old me, who needs you to get through today and tomorrow, and the next forty or fifty years, I am furious, and I want to lay you across my lap and tan your damned behind." She smiled a sad smile. I said, "I am making light of it, but I mean every damned word of it."

"I'm sorry. I just saw what was happening and had to act."

I sighed. "It's who you are, and it's why I love you. Just try not to die before I do, okay?"

"Deal."

By the time we got to the Jacobi, Abdo had been admitted, and his surgeon, an efficient Arian android by the name of Dr. Ingrid Weiss, was waiting for the results of an emergency pre-op. Outside his room she told us, "He is staple"—she meant stable but she said "staple"—"ant there is no risk, but he is very weak ant you must not exhaust him before de operation."

Dehan asked, "But we can talk to him?"

"One or two questions, but not de heavy interrogation, please."

We pushed into his room. He was in bed and looked an unhealthy yellow-brown color. When he saw Dehan, there was hatred in his eyes. His voice came as a croak.

"My hand is long, woman. Whatever you do to me, I will reach you. I will reach out and touch you, and I will kill you."

She glanced at me and smiled, and we drew up a chair to each side of his bed. I spoke quietly.

"Abdo, we are only here to ask you a couple of questions. Before we start, I want you to understand something about American prisons. Whatever you think you can do from the inside out, we can do from the outside in. Only on the inside, it's worse. So you come after my partner, and you'll have thirty guys coming for you inside. So watch your step."

Dehan asked him, "You ready to cooperate? The more you help us now, the more it will be reflected in sentencing."

He was quiet so long I thought he wasn't going to answer, but finally he said, "What do you want to know?"

She drew breath to ask, but I beat her to it because I knew we only had a couple of questions. I said, "What is your problem with Buddhism?"

The look of contempt on his face told me everything I needed to know.

"What you are talking about, stupid son of fuckin' dog? Allah is only god, Mohamed is his prophet, *Allahu Akbar!*"

Dehan glanced at me with a small frown. To Abdo she said, "You killed Ana Orcera, why did you do that?"

He sneered. "Ana? Ana was stupid, fuckin' *eahira*! Like you. Is long time ago. You stupid dogs are still looking for killer? American *alqarf*!"

Dehan shook her head. "No, we found the killer. We just want to know why you did it?"

"Fuck you."

"How about Mathew Cavendish? You remember him? 2016. You killed him too. You couldn't tie the knots right and made a mess."

"You full of shit."

"Why'd you kill him? What had he done to you?"

He closed his eyes. "I am weak. Leave me alone. You shoot me just because I am Arab. You fuckin' filthy prejudice, Jew-loving American *eahira*. Allah will punish. Your blood will flow like river. God will punish. *Allahu Akbar!*"

After that we could get nothing more out of him, and a busy nurse with a disapproving mouth came and started fussing and glaring at us, so we left.

Down in the parking lot, dawn was breaking gray across the horizon, making the air cool and the streetlamps that still lingered look pale and ineffectual. Dehan stopped after a couple of strides and turned to look at me.

"What was that?"

"You'll have to be a bit more precise."

"'What is your problem with Buddhism?' Seriously? It's not exactly inspired interrogation, Sensei. And also, you threatened him, Stone. If anybody had heard you . . ."

I put a hand on her shoulder. "Dehan, that is two questions. And they do not, together, constitute a 'that.'"

"What the hell are you talking about?"

"You asked me, 'What was that?' And 'that' was two completely unconnected things. First, if any guy threatens to hurt you, I will do whatever it takes to protect you, and I don't care what laws I break or who hears me. That is just the way it is."

She smiled a nice smile and said, "Oh."

"As to my uninspired question, what can I say? Perhaps Sensei grow old, Little Grasshopper."

"Yeah, sure. It was a dumb question, Stone, and you don't ask dumb questions, because dumb questions beget dumb answers."

I turned and propelled her gently toward the car.

"Perhaps I wasn't really interested in his answer."

She stopped and screwed up her face at me. "So what the hell's the point in asking a question if you're not interested in the answer?"

"That," I said, and wagged a finger at her, "is an extremely good question!"

"I want to kill you when you get like this."

I unlocked the door of the old Jag and leaned on the roof. "I, on the other hand," I said, "want to go and have a much more thorough look at the profiles of the other victims. We have a big problem, Dehan." I wagged my key at her. "Or you have. Abdo is not going to cooperate. He is going to make us work. And you are going to have to prove a connection between him and each of the six victims. That is not going to be easy. Okay, we know he drives a cab, and we can speculate that he has at some time or other given a ride to the victims. But that is just speculation, and we cannot prove it. Further, the MO in these killings does not fit the rest of his profile. The murders we can get him on are contract killings or killings in the sadomasochistic setting of prostitution. But the six murders we are investigating are almost ritualistic—and the music, Dehan, the sacred music. This is not the *azaan* he is playing them. He is playing them Christian sacred music,

Buddhist meditation, and Zen music. It is going to be very hard for you to link him to those killings."

"Difficult for *me*..."

I grinned. "I am happy to send him down for the guns, the drugs, the rape and torture, the prostitutes, and the contract killings. But I am not convinced he killed Jensen and the other five."

She leaned across the roof and pointed her finger at me. "He's the guy! You are overlooking the obvious because you are getting hung up on the whole philosophical side of this. But I keep telling you, it's a smoke screen. This son of a bitch likes to play games. You want explanations for the music? Fine! How's this? Ana Orcera, constantly seeking some kind of spiritual shortcut to happiness. She had just gone from Protestant to Catholic, refusing along the way to convert to Islam. So he kills her and plays the music of salvation to *mock* her!" She held up two fingers. "Mathew Cavendish, an atheist flirting with Buddhism, another one seeking a quasi-religious path to follow. He was played Zen music, Epstein described it as weird and jerky, remember? What does an atheist flirting with Buddhism sound like to a Muslim fundamentalist? Weird and jerky fits the bill for me. Again, the music was to *mock* him! Saul Arender, a Jewish lawyer defending criminals. He got Tibetan bells. Maybe they represented the Christian bells of the people he defended. I don't know, but again it was *mockery*, Stone. Judge Jones, Gregorian chants, *mocking*! Georgina Cheng, the vivisectionist, English Tudor music ... The last one, Jensen, Renaissance music, mocking the Buddhist who is still at heart a Christian. All that music is, Stone, is mockery. It's the work of a person with an imperfect understanding of Western culture, and for that very reason it looks like a puzzle. But it's not a puzzle, it's the ineffectual mockery of an idiot."

I pursed my lips and gently tapped my key on the roof of the car. "Mockery," I said.

"Yeah! Mockery. You are a smart guy, Stone, probably one of the smartest people I ever met, and you have a really intelligent way of thinking. But not everybody is like you. Most people are kind of dumb, and people who go around killing other people for kicks are *real* dumb. People who think philosophically, and call thinking epistemology, and morals ethics, usually don't go around killing people. They're too busy thinking."

The barrage had subsided into an almost apologetic explanation. Her face said this was something that most people understood intuitively, and the only reason I didn't get it was because I was so smart. I smiled at her.

"I hadn't thought about it like that."

"He's the guy, Stone. He killed Ana and got the taste for it. Then he killed the rest and had a gas playing crazy music for them."

I sighed noisily. "Okay, but what I said still holds, Little Grasshopper: you still have to prove it."

"Yeah . . ." She grinned. "I know."

We climbed in, and I backed out of the lot. Dehan had the window down and was drumming her fingers on the door. "What do you want to do?" she said.

"I know what you want to do."

She arched an eyebrow. "Really? What?"

"You want to go to the warehouse and see what Joe has found there."

"Don't you?"

"Not a whole lot, no. I have a proposition for you."

"Darling, I thought you'd never ask."

I smiled at her. "That was funny, Dehan. That was witty. You're a witty woman."

"What's your proposition, smart-ass?"

"Breakfast, give the team time to do their work, and then you go and investigate the warehouse and I will go and talk to somebody I am very interested in talking to?"

She scowled. "Who? And why can't I come?"

"Because you want to prove that Abdo Deng done it and I don't."

She gave a big, short sigh, said, "But how can you not . . ." and sagged back in her seat, then said, "Stone . . . ? *He killed Ana!* And whoever killed Ana killed the other five!"

"I know, I know. I agree, but I just need to satisfy myself about something."

"What? Or rather who?"

I grunted. "I did a little research last night. Do you know how many times Saul Arender appeared before Judge Jeremiah Jones?"

She looked startled and stared at me. "No, never crossed my mind. How many?"

"Over a twenty-year career, entirely in the Bronx, he came up before him approximately two hundred times."

"Huh . . ." She turned and stared out at Morris Park Avenue, yawning and stretching in the early morning. "Is that important?"

"Probably not, but it tells us there is a connection between the two of them. They knew each other. Maybe they even played golf together."

"Huh . . ." she said again without looking at me. "So, seeing as they are both dead these past two and three years, who is it you are going to see?"

Emilio's Pizza was approaching on the right. He always opened for the early breakfast trade, and he made the best coffee for many miles around, and by far the best ciambella this side of Rome. I pulled up outside and killed the engine.

"The person I am really keen to talk to is Saul Arender's secretary."

TWELVE

Saul Arender's secretary was a thin man of indeterminate age. He was definitely more than twenty-two, and definitely less than fifty-five, but beyond that it was impossible to be either precise or confident. He had a spherical head with sandy hair that was as lacking in definition as his age. When remembering him, you were not sure whether he was bald, receding, or had a full head of very thin hair parted to the side. Equally you were not sure if he had a moustache and glasses or whether he was clean-shaven.

One thing that was certain about him was that he wore a suit. It was a three-piece, charcoal gray with a very fine stripe. It was well cut, off the peg, and very old.

He now worked for Sean Shave and Sheering on West 44th, and agreed to meet me at the Europa on 6th Avenue. I pushed through the plate glass doors and found him sitting at a small, red plastic table with a paper bucket of cappuccino in front of him. He stood as I approached and offered me something that was more the memory of a smile than the ghost.

"If you don't mind, I'll dispense with the whole elbow farce. The clasp and shake of a hand means something, as do the expressions . . ." He made circular motions around his face with his finger. ". . . of our faces. But we have been robbed of both, and I prefer not to pander to their cynicism. The hand or nothing. How do you do? I am Edgar Levi."

He offered me his hand, and I shook it. We sat, and I showed him my badge.

"I am Detective John Stone."

"You have to identify yourself, I understand. You are investigating the deaths of Mr. Arender and His Honor Judge Jones, among others."

"That's right."

He seemed to like to be in control of what was said, so I waited for him to go on. He stared at the red tabletop, rubbing his thumbs with his fingertips. The espresso machine screamed, and the door thudded open, allowing in a waft of cool air.

"The investigating detective at the time was not very interested in what I had to say. I hope you are not offended by emotion. It is still very upsetting to remember. I found him, you know."

I nodded that I knew. "I am not offended by emotion, Mr. Levi. Please, go ahead."

"I entered the office that morning as usual at seven a.m. I usually put in at least a couple of hours' work before Mr. Arender turned up. He would turn up at between nine and ten. Then I would brief him for the day over coffee and . . ." He trailed off. "Anyway, you are not interested in the trivia. That was our routine. But that morning when I opened up and went into his office . . ." He shook his head in quick little jerks. "I pray to God I never have to see anything like that again. He had been hanged, but his murderer had engineered an improvised gallows that tightened the cord around his neck every time he moved his body. So the more he attempted to escape, the tighter the cord drew about his throat."

"So he had been there all night."

"It would seem so. I had left at six the previous evening, and he was still there. He said he had a private meeting and told me to leave."

"You have no idea whom the meeting was with?"

"None whatever. The appointment was not made through me, and as I understand it—you would know this better than I—the laboratory investigation of his telephone found no calls that were in any way helpful. All the calls logged on his phone for the previous forty-eight hours were accounted for. So the arrangement was either made on a burner, by post, or in person."

"But according to the file, no burner was ever found. How much do you know about his personal life?"

He gave a small shrug with thin shoulders. "I know he hardly had one. He was divorced but devoted to his wife and his children. He was a mensch, a good father and a good husband whose only failing was that he worked too hard to provide for his family. He was either at the office or he was with his wife and children. Sometimes I wondered why they bothered to get divorced."

"No affairs . . . ?"

"No, no, no . . ."

"What about involvement with crooks? Were there people leaning on him for special favors, anything like that?"

"Always, but he was a very smart man. He had insurance on all the clients who could prove problematic. He recorded every interview, even filmed them sometimes. It is not widely known, but when Mr. Arender died, a whole lot of people were prosecuted and went to prison because of the files that were automatically sent to the DA."

I smiled. "That is satisfying to know." The door opened again, and a chill breeze snaked around my ankles. The fall was approaching, laced cold into the air. The door clunked closed again, and a voice called, *"Due cappuccini!"*

I said, "What's your theory?"

"I have wondered. For three years I have wondered. I know about the others. Ana Orcera, Mr. Cavendish, Georgina Cheng . .

. and now Mr. Jensen. They seem to be punishments of a particularly cruel type."

I frowned. "Punishments?"

He was thoughtful for a while. Then, "My mother would often punish me. Usually it was a slap on the back of my head. If it was something more serious, then she would take her slipper to me. Little was ever said. I knew what I had done wrong, punishment was dispensed, and that was the end of it.

"However, if my father punished me, the punishment was not enough. He, like the God of biblical times, wanted repentance. He wanted me to know the reason for the punishment, he wanted to explain it to me, he wanted me to know it was my fault, and he wanted me to meditate on all of that while he punished me. And it would invariably end with the words, 'See? That's what you get!' This killer reminds me of my father. He wants to punish these people for some perceived wrong, and he wants them to know why they are dying, and he wants them to think about it until the moment of death. The music he plays is his version of 'See? That's what you get.'"

"That's very perceptive."

"Thank you. I have had time to think about it."

"Does anyone come to mind?"

He smiled briefly, and for just a moment his face was transformed. "The district attorney."

I laughed, and slowly the smile decayed and slipped away.

"Certainly the DA had reason to resent Mr. Arender. He was an extremely good defense lawyer. He was electrifying on his feet, eloquent, charismatic, totally committed to each case. The DA feared him, and the juries loved him. But I can't honestly think of anyone who would want to do that to him."

I leaned back in my chair and drummed my fingers on the table. "What did you make of the actual method of execution? Did that mean anything to you? I mean, he was basically executing himself, wasn't he?"

"Yes. But more than that I saw it as the killer telling him that he was a prisoner of his own actions."

I felt a chill run up my arms and my back, and a sensation like the roots of my hair were moving.

"A prisoner of his own actions . . ."

"He was gaining freedom for people who didn't deserve it, but his attempts to gain his own freedom would lead to his own death."

He nodded. "Something like that. He was being punished for defending criminals. That is how I read it." He took a deep breath and sighed. "But . . ."

I echoed his nod and said, "But then, a year later, we have Judge Jeremiah Jones, Three Jay."

"He was what used to be known as a hanging judge." He gestured at me with an open hand. "You are a policeman with many years of experience. I know you, though you probably didn't know me, and Mr. Arender was well aware of you. So you know what His Honor Mr. Jones was like. If you were found guilty, you could expect the most severe penalty available to the law. His view was, if you broke the law, you had to be punished." He spread his hands and flopped them on the table one on top of the other. "So he wants criminals to have no legal defense, but he doesn't want them punished either?"

I made a noise of agreement. "How well did Mr. Arender and Judge Jones know each other?"

"Very well. They were friends. They'd known each other for years. They dined together, went to each other's kids' birthdays . . ." He shook his head, remembering. "People said His Honor was a Republican, right-wing Christian fundamentalist. But he was no such thing. He was a very broad-minded intellectual who had very clear ideas about crime and punishment. He passed a few severe sentences in his time, and everybody in the courtroom, including Mr. Arender and his client, knew that the accused deserved it. But I have also watched him pass lenient and enlightened sentences when he knew that the accused needed a second chance, and that it would not be wasted. Those sentences don't get reported, because they don't sell papers."

He took a sip of his coffee and set it down carefully on the table. "And then," he said, "the other four murders have nothing whatever to do with the law. I wondered for a while if it was a clever ruse: to make it look like a serial killer to confuse the police, when in fact there are one or two genuine targets mixed in with the apparently random selection made by the putative serial killer. Like that movie with Tom Cruise."

"You think the intended victims might have been the judge or Mr. Arender?"

"Or Georgina Cheng. People get very hot under the collar about vivisection, as you know."

I made a noncommittal noise and said, "I have just a couple more questions, Mr. Levi. As I understand it, Mr. Arender was not so much a nonpracticing Jew as overworked."

"I'd say that was accurate, yes."

"So, what I am wondering about is the choice of music. Tibetan bells. Would Tibetan bells mean anything to Mr. Arender?"

He sat back in his chair with both hands on the table, and his sight became abstracted.

"That's interesting," he said at last. "You associate the music with the victim; I always associated it with the killer. I always assumed the killer had some kind of obsession with spiritual music. But I suppose it makes more sense your way. The music is picked to fit the victim."

I nodded. "So why Tibetan bells?"

"He had recently defended a very rough character. He had been in the marines, seen active duty, was a very violent man to whom the marines had not managed to teach self-discipline. He had trained in various types of martial arts, was constantly getting into violent altercations, and had done time. Shortly before he came to us, it seems the martial arts had led him to Tao and then Buddhism, and he was trying to reform and find inner peace.

However, when he stopped to meditate, as it were, his past caught up with him, and he was prosecuted for stabbing a man repeatedly with a bowie knife in a bar fight. He came and sought Mr. Arender's help. He claimed that of all the crimes he had rightly been accused of, in this case it genuinely was self-defense."

Again the door behind me swung open and let in chill air, and with it the sound of pattering, hissing rain.

"What happened?"

"Mr. Arender fought the case on the grounds of self-defense and that William Corder was a reformed man who had, before the fight, sought the path of peace. It helped that the knife was not his, but his assailant's. There were witnesses willing to testify that Mr. Corder had been quietly taking a drink when the man assaulted him. He was acquitted but cautioned to stay out of trouble."

"How does this lead us to Tibetan bells?"

"Ah, yes. Mr. Corder and Mr. Arender formed something of a friendship. He, Mr. Corder, was crude and somewhat aggressive, but also intelligent and remarkably deep. He invited Mr. Arender to a number of exhibitions related to Buddhism. Mr. Corder's style, so to speak, was not Tibetan, but they went to an exhibition, or a demonstration, of Tibetan bells, and Mr. Arender was deeply impressed. I recall that he told me it transcended religion and touched the human spirit."

I was quiet for a long moment, aware that I had heard something of extreme importance, but unable yet to place it into context. All I could say was, "That is remarkable . . ."

He nodded, like he agreed with me, but said, "Is it?"

"Have you any contact details for this William Corder?"

He shook his head. "I imagine Mr. Arender had his number. Perhaps his wife has his address book. But he was very much a drifter. It was three years ago. He could be anywhere."

"Yeah, I'll talk to Mr. Arender's ex-wife." I drew breath to thank him but stopped and hesitated. "You said that Mr. Corder's style of Buddhism was not Tibetan. Do you remember what it was?"

Again his gaze became abstracted, and he looked out the window at the wet, crawling traffic and the milling millions of people, hunched under their umbrellas.

"There are quite a few styles, aren't there?" He spoke quietly, to the window. "I know Zen is a form of Buddhism, but that's from Japan, isn't it. And there is Chinese Buddhism, or there was. I don't know if it survives. If I recall, from the conversations they had, it started in India, Buddha was Indian. Is that right? I am trying to remember."

I nodded. "Yes, he was an Indian prince."

"Gautama, something like that. But then it spread out of India to China and Tibet, and Japan and Indonesia, and India reverted to Hinduism. I know that he claimed his style was the most pure and preserved the original teachings, but I suppose they all say that, don't they? And then there are other Buddhas that have come along since him."

"You don't recall anything special about his style? Where did they meet? Was there a temple where he went to meditate, or to study?"

He sighed deeply and shook his head.

"I am an atheist, Detective Stone," he said at last. "I have no interest in religion, hope, or salvation." He looked at me. "I am with Sir Walter Raleigh: death is the cure to all ills. So I don't really recall many details of their conversations, which held little interest for me, but I do seem to remember that his form of Buddhism originated in Sri Lanka. I'm not sure if that helps at all."

"Yes." I nodded. "That helps."

I offered him my hand, we shook, and I left.

Outside, I hunched into my shoulders and loped through the rain toward my old, burgundy Jag.

THIRTEEN

I SAT BEHIND THE WHEEL FOR A WHILE, WATCHING 6TH
Avenue warp wetly through rain on my windshield. Eventually I
called Dehan.

"Hey, how's it hanging? You wet yet? You spoke to Arender's
secretary?"

"Yup."

"Was it a waste of time?"

"Nope."

"I was afraid you'd say that, but I also knew that you would."

"How about you?"

"I gotta tell you, Stone, I think you're on a wild goose chase.
We have enough on this guy to hang him six times over."

"Anything to connect him with the other victims?"

"Not directly, but one of his pals a few years back was
sentenced by Three Jay. Went down for fifteen years."

"Was he defended by Arender?"

A small laugh. "Yeah, that's what I thought, but it wasn't him.
So you on your way back?"

I was quiet for a moment, then I said, "Yeah, listen, do something for me, will you? I need you to get me the number for Judge
Jones' widow. When you've done that, I need you to contact

Georgina Cheng's next of kin, failing that, close friends or colleagues, and find out if she had any contact or connection with Buddhism." And as an afterthought I added, "Or if anyone close to her was a Buddhist."

"You won't let go, huh? Stone, we have him."

"I'm sure you're right, Dehan. But I need to see where this thread leads. And so far, you haven't connected Abdo Deng with anyone but Ana Orcera."

"Okay." Then she added, "You want to know where we're at?"

"I know we can't interrogate him."

"No, but we can interrogate Abdul Abbas and Farouk Bahjat."

"And they are?"

"The owners of fingerprints we found all over the heroin, the coke, and the crate of guns we found in the warehouse. They are both on FBI wanted lists suspected of terrorist connections."

I allowed a smile to creep into my voice. "Is either of them a Buddhist?"

"Maybe you can ask them yourself if you care to rejoin the investigation."

"Don't sulk, Dehan. It is unbecoming in a young lady of your standing. Get me that number, and chase up Georgina Cheng."

"Okay, then I am going to go and interrogate Farouk Bahjat. You want to be there for that?"

"I'll do my best."

"So where are you going to be?"

"I hope I'm going to be talking to Judge Jones' widow, if you'll stop badgering me and do what I asked."

"Jerk."

She hung up, and I headed slowly, through wet, stop-start traffic, toward Madison Avenue Bridge, and finally across the river and through the concrete spaghetti of Mott Haven and Port Morris eventually to connect with the Bruckner Expressway. By the time I had got to Longwood, Dehan called.

"Where are you?"

"Crawling along the expressway. What have you got?"

"Mrs. Fiona Jones' telephone number and address. Apparently she had complained several times in influential but unofficial circles that the investigation into her husband's death has not made more progress. You going to tell her nobody has realized till now it's all about Buddhists seeking for truth?"

"Is that the clanking of a closed mind I hear?"

"Let me know when you decide to come home, darling."

I came off at Exit 52 onto the Bruckner Boulevard and continued to Soundview, where I turned south. The traffic wasn't so heavy, but the rain was, and the wipers were working hard to keep my windshield clear. The sky had turned dark, and wherever you looked on the sidewalk, people were scuttling for cover. Eventually, at Shorehaven, I turned into Cornell Avenue, a short road that ended in a footpath that led down to the river. Right now, the whole thing was shrouded in a mist of raindrops pounding off the buildings and the blacktop and drumming on the roof of my car. But through the mist, on the left, I could see a large, white clapboard building, which gave the impression of several houses that had been knocked into one. It had gabled roofs on two or three levels, bow windows, and stained glass above a large, white double door and set decoratively into the upper floors.

I sat looking at it for a while, then dialed the number Dehan had given me. A cute voice with a hint of Latino said, "Mrs. Jones' residence. How may I help you?"

"This is Detective John Stone, NYPD. I'd like to talk to Mrs. Jones, please."

"One momen' please."

It was closer to a minute than a moment, but eventually an entirely different kind of voice came on the line. It was the kind of voice the English call an "empire builder's voice." She might have been a Brit who'd spent many years in the States, or she might have been an East Coast American with a family tree on her wall leading all the way back to English blue bloods.

"Mrs. Jeremiah Jones speaking," she said.

"Mrs. Jones, this is Detective John Stone of the New York Police Department. I wonder if you could spare a few moments to answer some questions about your husband."

"Oh, you have finally decided to do something about that, have you? It's a little late in the day, isn't it? I had understood that evidence goes cold after a short while. My husband was murdered two years ago."

"Yes, ma'am, that is true. We are a cold-case unit based at the Forty-Third Precinct. The case was very recently handed to us. Do you mind answering a couple of questions over the telephone?"

"I don't mind doing anything that will assist in the capture of my husband's killer. I only wish *somebody* would do *something* to catch him."

"I understand, Mrs. Jones. Was your husband a close friend of an attorney by the name of Saul Arender?"

"Yes, of course, Saul and Rachel were both good friends of ours. Poor Saul was murdered just the year before, and nothing was done about that either!"

"Mrs. Jones, I need you to think carefully about this. Shortly before he died, Saul Arender became interested in various aspects of Buddhism . . ."

"Oh my good Lord!"

I paused, momentarily thrown off my track by her reaction, but before I could continue, she stormed on.

"He, a good Jew, became *obsessed* with it. Now, I am a Christian, and my ancestors were Puritans, and I know Christianity has not always viewed the Jews with favor. But we are far more enlightened now, and I am very much in favor of the Jews. Our religions are fraternal, we both pray to the same god, Jehovah, and we hold the same values of charity and love thy neighbor. I believe a good Christian should remain a good Christian, and a good Jew should be a good Jew. But Saul, a man I have always respected deeply, suddenly started banging on about dhamma and karma and the Lord knows what other unpronounceable nonsense . . ."

I stepped in. "Did the judge share your view of Buddhism?"

She sighed. "No, I am afraid he did not. He was not as enthusiastic as Saul, but he was definitely interested, and they went to several exhibitions together, and even a short course on one occasion."

I looked out of the window, where the rain was forming brown puddles on the lawn.

"Where were those exhibitions and the course held, Mrs. Jones? Can you remember?"

"Of course. There is nothing wrong with my memory, Detective Stone. Two of the exhibitions were at the Museum of Oriental Art and Culture, on Amsterdam Avenue, in Manhattan. Then there was a concert and an exhibition of sculpture, and both of those and the course were at the Bronx Vihara, at, let me think . . ."

I said, "210 Cornell Avenue, Shorehaven."

"Yes, exactly."

"Thank you, Mrs. Jones, you have been extremely helpful."

"Is that it?" She sounded disappointed.

I nodded, though she couldn't see me. "Yes," I said. "For now, that's it. Though we may have to talk to you again soon, if that's okay."

"Of course . . ." There was a moment's silence, then, "You think you have something?"

"I don't know, Mrs. Jones. We are investigating. I'll let you know if there is any kind of development."

"Fobbed off again," she said, but she sounded happier than when she had first answered the telephone.

I hung up, climbed out of the car, and ran along the concrete path toward the big doors to the Bronx Vihara. Seven steps carried me to the shelter of the porch. There I realized that the stained glass fan above the door was in fact an image of the Buddha seated in the lotus position at the center of a giant lotus flower. I was about to ring the bell but noticed a sign above it that said, *The door is open, please come in.* So I turned the handle and stepped inside.

I was in a large, dark hall with a broad staircase that made a right angle from the wall on my left and up the wall in front of me, to disappear out of view. Against that far wall, beneath the stairs, was a water feature about five feet across, depicting the Buddha sitting on a lotus flower in a pond. The image of the Buddha was large, about three and a half feet high, in the lotus position, with an expression of absolute peace, which was accentuated by the soft music that was playing in the background.

On my left there was a mahogany door with a sign over it that read *Meditation Room*. On my right, and slightly behind me, was another door. Over that one a sign proclaimed it to be the library.

I peered inside but found nothing but a couple of thousand books and a sign that invited me to take any book I liked and leave a donation, as large or small as I pleased. I stood in the doorway and looked around. There were several comfortable chairs. A table at the center held leaflets and magazines. Large bookcases lined the walls, but for the bay window that overlooked the lawn, Cornell Avenue, and the river on the left.

A voice made me turn.

"Can I help you?"

The voice belonged to a man standing across the room in the shadows. He was of indeterminate age, probably over forty. He was bald, his skin was dark, and his nose was large and slightly hooked. He was dressed in a saffron robe. His eyes were large and intense, and very dark.

I showed him my badge. "I'm Detective John Stone, NYPD. I was hoping to talk to whoever is in charge."

His smile was almost apologetic.

"Nobody is in charge, Detective." A hint of mischief crept into his face. "We work toward seeing things as they really are, Detective, and power and authority are, after all, only illusions."

I nodded and returned the smile. "But the mortgage and the monthly bills, unfortunately, are not. Who pays them?"

He gave a small bow. "We have a head monk, Bodhisattva Adhiṭṭhāna, but I wouldn't say he was in charge, exactly. However, he does pay the bills and the mortgage, and at times he guides our steps when our minds grow confused."

"Can I speak to him?"

"I don't know, but I can tell him you are here, and I am sure he will come and listen to you."

"Thank you . . ." I hesitated a moment. He waited, and I said, "You are a monk?"

"Yes, normal people don't dress like this."

I smiled. "In the Theravada tradition?"

"Yes." This time his answer was slower, accompanied by a slow nod.

"What . . ." I began, and trailed off. "What is the defining feature of Theravada Buddhism, as opposed to all the other styles and disciplines?"

He dropped his gaze from my face to the floor and stood a long while in silence. Finally he said, "The purpose of Buddhism, of any school or style, is to stop pain and suffering by the attainment of enlightenment. In Theravada we focus on attaining liberation from samsara, the eternal cycle of life, death, and rebirth, by one's own efforts." He paused. "Because, when we die, our final thoughts condition our next becoming, training the mind in meditation and concentration are essential for the path to enlightenment. It is an important part of Buddhism to die with the right state of mind."

He waited a moment. I nodded, and he smiled and bowed, turning to leave. I took a step. "What is your name?"

He turned again to face me. "Bhavana Dhana. I will go now and find Bhante Bodhisattva Adhiṭṭhāna. Please"—he gestured to the small library and bowed again—"feel free to wait in the library, and read if you are curious."

I had to resist the urge to bow back, and withdrew into the room.

I waited for about ten minutes, reading *Mindfulness in Plain*

English, by Bhante Henepola Gunaratana. I didn't hear him arrive, but I sensed his presence at the door and looked up. He was in his sixties, in good shape, maybe six foot or a little more, with a humorous face, kind eyes, a gray beard, and long, fine white hair. He looked more like Gandalf than a Buddhist monk, but maybe that was just my mistaken perception.

He smiled. "Detective John Stone?"

I stood. "I'm sorry, I don't recall your name, but you are the head monk?"

"I am, Samuel Ogden." He must have caught the surprise in my face because he laughed. "I have a much more complicated, euphonious one for my dhamma name in Pali, Bodhisattva Adhiṭṭhāna, but that is more a statement of aspiration, or intention, than a descriptive epithet."

I nodded. "Not a descriptive epithet, but a statement of intent."

He answered the nod and crossed the room toward me. I realized for the first time that he was wearing saffron robes. He placed a hand on my shoulder and gestured. "Let's sit here, and you can tell me how I can help you."

I sat on a small sofa with my back to the bay window. He sat on a chair at right angles to the sofa and leaned his elbows on his knees to look at me. His eyes were penetrating and blue, and I was aware that though they were rich in compassion, there was no weakness about them.

"I am not sure if you can help me . . ." I hesitated. "Bhante?"

He smiled. "Bhante is a term of respect, like master, or you can call me bhikkhu, it just means monk. But by all means call me Sam or Mr. Ogden, or Dr. Ogden, or whatever you are most comfortable with. What we call a thing does not change its nature. Now, tell me, how do you think I might not be able to help you?"

I nodded. "Thank you. We are investigating a series of murders that occurred over the last six years. The case has repeatedly gone cold and finally landed up on my desk, at the cold-cases unit. Nobody had ever got very far with it, but I happened to notice that of the six victims, five had some kind of connection with this vihara, and that was the *only* thing they had in common."

For a moment there was an expression of extreme sadness on his face, but it passed, like a cloud over a summer beach. He nodded very slowly.

"I am very sorry to hear that. A vihara is an instrument of peace and of compassion. To hear that it has in some way been connected with murder is very upsetting. In what way were these people connected with the vihara?"

"Each one in a different way. It is very hard to make sense of it. Perhaps if I tell you their names and a little bit about them, you might remember something . . ."

"I am quite sure I will."

"The first, I am going back a bit, was a woman by the name of Ana Orcera." He frowned. I went on. "She was a single mother who, according to what I have been able to gather, was searching for some kind of spiritual meaning in her life. She got involved with a lot of groups and wound up returning to the Catholic Church by way of the Church of Divine Grace and Rebirth . . ."

"On Leland Avenue?"

I nodded. "That's right."

He closed his eyes. "This was about six years ago. She was a lively, attractive young woman, slightly overweight. I seem to remember she was sincere, a little afraid, and"—he laughed—"terribly lazy."

"Afraid?" He watched me and nodded a couple of times, like he was waiting for me to finish a question. I said, "What of? Afraid of what?"

"She spoke to me privately a few times. She was craving attention. The impression I got was that she was afraid of her boyfriend, and she was afraid of Reverend Wells, but most of all she was afraid of being abandoned and left alone. That is why she tolerated so much."

"So much of what?"

Again he paused to watch me. There was amusement in his eyes, like he found it funny that I was so blind.

"I'm sure you know that her boyfriend . . ." He waited a second, staring at the floor. "Ab . . . Abdo Deng, from the Sudan, I believe, I am sure you know that he was a very violent man who used to abuse her and her son. He beat them both and caused them great pain. Few mothers would tolerate that kind of man in their house. But she did because the fear of being left alone was stronger than the fear of what he might do to her or her son. She was very scared and unhappy. She also tolerated a different kind of abuse from Reverend Wells."

"What kind of abuse?"

He smiled, then grimaced. "Being a spiritual guide is an invidious path that is plagued with dangers. The first and greatest of these is the desire to make everybody who comes to you follow *your* path, rather than their own. There are as many paths to enlightenment, Detective, as there are people seeking it. Reverend Morton Wells, a very honorable and decent man, I am sure, has a very powerful personality, and from what poor Ana told me, he could be a little overbearing, hectoring, and controlling. He was very fond of her . . . I encouraged her to take responsibility for her life and seek happiness. I believe he encouraged her to seek God, through him."

"How fond?"

"I can only tell you what she told me in confidence, and that was that she felt he had become too fond of her on a personal level. She felt that he had become too involved in her personal life and was attempting to control it. But I stress, I have no personal experience of that. Ultimately, Detective, as I am quite sure you know, we are each of us responsible for our own lives. We cannot help a soul that does not want to be helped. Sadly, that was something Ana was having trouble understanding. She wanted to be free to do as she pleased, but she wanted everybody else to be responsible."

I thought about that for a moment, then said, "A year later, Mathew Cavendish . . ."

"Oh, I remember Mathew very well. He was a highly intelligent man with a powerful, intuitive grasp of the fundamental principles of Buddhism. Very much an individualist, and struggled deeply to detach himself from the idea of *atman*."

"*Atman?* I'm sorry, what is that?"

"It is a principle in Hindu philosophy that says that the 'I' is a unique, indestructible self at the heart of each person. Buddha said that this was not so, that with enlightenment the ego is snuffed out, like a flame on a candle. Mathew found that very hard to accept."

"He came here often?"

"Oh yes, often and regularly. He studied on several courses and joined our meditation group. He was a superb student, sincere, dedicated, and intelligent."

"What made him leave?"

"He came to talk to me about becoming a monk. I advised him against it. As I said to you before, Buddhism is not evangelical. We do not seek to convert people. You can be a good Catholic or a Jew, and still practice Buddhism. Buddhism in essence is simply compassion, loving kindness, and the search for truth. My feeling, from Mathew, was that he should continue exploring and investigating, so I advised him to explore the Tao, psychoanalysis, anything that would help him get to grips with the understanding that the self is simply a finite series of processes."

I was surprised, and my face said so. "Finite?"

"Over many, many lifetimes, Detective, if we finally reach enlightenment, the little ego, the *idea* of self, is snuffed out like a candle."

"He didn't like that idea."

"It is a very hard concept to grasp. The self believes itself to be indestructible, and violently rejects anything that threatens its integrity. After all, the loss of self is death."

FOURTEEN

THE RAIN HAD PICKED UP OUTSIDE AND WAS RATTLING hard at the glass in the window in sudden gusts, then receding to bow the tops of the trees in the street outside. Sam Ogden stood and went to the door, where he flipped a switch and several lamps came on. They cast more light but did little to dispel the gloom. As I watched him sit, I asked, "Did Ana and Mathew Cavendish have any contact with each other?"

He shook his head. "No, none at all."

"Okay, the next two victims were Saul Arender and Judge Jeremiah Jones . . ."

"I remember them very well. They were both highly intelligent men. Judge Jones was more cautious, his approach was more intellectual and analytical, but Saul's was more emotional. He really felt that he had found an answer. Saul was very intense, very passionate."

"Bhikkhu, can you think of any connection, however tenuous, between these four people, other than the obvious one that they each had some connection with this vihara?"

His answer was immediate and unhesitating. "No, but who are the remaining two people?"

"Reginald Jensen."

"Ah, yes, I heard about Reginald. And who is the other?"

"Georgina Cheng . . ."

"The vivisectionist?"

"Yes."

"She had no connection with this vihara, Detective Stone. We do not support cruelty and mutilation, even in the name of science and medicine."

"That's what I thought. They are not exactly compatible pursuits."

He smiled. "You'd be surprised at the people who do turn to Buddhism, though. Dhamma has a way of making itself felt, even in the darkest places where light cannot penetrate, yet somehow the mind sees its own light. Buddhism teaches that we must not kill, it teaches that we must have compassion and empathy for all sentient beings, but it does not close the door to people who have killed or been cruel in the past. It does not close the door to those who continue to kill and continue to be actively cruel. The truth does not belong to Buddhism, but a good Buddhist helps others to find the truth, and with it freedom from suffering and pain." He held my eye and gestured at the books around us. "That is why we cannot charge for these books, but ask instead for a donation, because the dhamma belongs to no one, and is for everyone. Nobody has a monopoly on truth, Detective. Truth is all there is."

The certainty of his words and the absolute clarity with which he delivered them was almost hypnotic, and I felt for a moment that I had been adrift for years in a dark sea, and had momentarily glimpsed the light of a distant harbor.

I drew breath and pressed on. "So you can't tell me of any connection between these five—or six—people that you are aware of?"

"You say they were all murdered? I knew poor Reggie had been murdered. I had no idea his death was connected to all these others. I will meditate on it, Detective. And if anything comes to me, I will of course contact you. It is intriguing that Georgina Cheng is the odd one out."

I gave a small laugh. "In fact, she is the only one who was born a Buddhist and converted, for want of a better word, to atheism."

"Oh." He raised his eyebrows. "That is interesting. So you had five non-Buddhists who became Buddhists or showed an interest in Buddhism, and one Buddhist who became an atheist." He frowned, and his face said that something was not satisfactory. "It seems very elaborate, doesn't it? I am no expert in criminology, believe me, but I believe serial killers tend to be of limited intelligence and, perhaps more to the point, deeply narcissistic. Yet your killer seems to have quite a complex mind, a philosophical bent, and, most important of all, he seems to be very interested in his victims. I would say they are almost more important than him."

That was a new angle to me, and I sank back in my seat to frown at him. "What makes you say that?"

He thought about it for a moment, like he wasn't sure himself why he had said it. "Well," he said at last, "for a start, there is the choice of victim. What is motivating him? Is it that they *are* Buddhists or that they are not? Clearly it is neither. Yet Buddhism is, according to what you have told me, the only element that connects them all. So your killer is selecting his victims according to . . ." He gave his head a small shake. "How can I express this? Some abstract quality of their minds? Whatever the case, he has made a very careful study of his victims and selected them on far more than a whim."

I hesitated a moment, trying to grasp what he was trying to tell me. He fixed me with his eyes, and I was suddenly aware of the intensity of his concentration. "These victims were selected intentionally, for a purpose. I think a serial killer kills for his own glorification. But this man kills for his victims."

I thanked him for his time and stepped out onto the wooden porch. I had rarely, if ever, met a man for whom I had so quickly felt such deep respect. He was in fact the first person I had met whose compassion and humanity was so readily palpable, but so completely unaffected.

I put up my collar and looked out at the rain. The downpour

had eased, and now there was a light drizzle falling from a pale gray sky, where pale blue rents showed fresh over the East River. I stood a moment, looking at the clarity in the sky, then picked my way across the sodden lawn to my car. I climbed in and slammed the door, sat staring at the droplets on the windshield, refracting reality and turning it upside down.

I called Dehan.

"Yeah, Stone. How's it going?"

I frowned. I hesitated to answer so long that she said, "Stone? You there?"

"Yeah, yeah, I'm here. Uh, I don't know. I think I just met a genuine saint."

"You *what*?"

"I said they all had a connection with Buddhism, Dehan. Each one of them. And all but one had a connection with the vihara. The one who didn't was Georgina Cheng. She was the reverse of all the others. She started out a Buddhist and gave it up; all the others were either born atheists or Christians, and either converted to Buddhism or developed a serious interest in it."

"Stone, what the hell are you talking about?"

"Listen to me, Dehan! Every single one of them had some connection with Buddhism and the Buddhist vihara."

"Stone . . ."

"It is too much of a coincidence. That is the one thing they all had in common. It is the one thing that connects them."

"Stone, listen to me . . ."

I felt a sudden rush of irritation. "Damn it, Dehan, I'm not some rookie who watches too much TV! I've been doing this for almost thirty years. I am not deluding myself with some crackpot theory! One thing and one thing alone connects these people! And that is Buddhism and the vihara, and each one of them was killed in a way that suggests the killer is obsessed with spiritual issues of redemption! That is not an unrealistic theory!"

She was quiet for a moment. Then she said, "No, it's not,

Stone, and I agree with you that it is a hell of a coincidence. But Deng has all but confessed."

I scowled at the wet trees in front of me.

"How? He's in the hospital, for crying out loud!"

"That was hours ago. It wasn't a complicated procedure. There was no major damage. When he came round, he said he wanted his lawyer . . ."

"What the hell does 'all but confessed' mean? He confessed or he didn't!"

"He's confessed to killing Ana, and he has admitted giving rides to the other five, including Georgina Cheng. So there is something else that connects them, besides Buddhism. Listen, you had better come to the hospital."

"I'm on my way."

I made a call to the TLC, then set off for the Jacobi. When I got there, Dehan was standing out on the steps outside reception with her hands in her pockets, watching me. I parked, and as I approached her through the drizzle, she said, "Your hair's wet. If I smoked, I'd smoke right now. This guy is giving it up like somebody stuck a canary so far up his ass its head's come out his mouth."

"Let's see if we can make sense of the words he's singing. Where is he?"

She led me to his room, and I found him sitting up with a drip in his arm and sipping orange juice. The whites of his eyes had a yellow hue, and his skin looked sallow. He had his head back against the pillow and his eyes closed. On his left was a guy in a suit. He wore heavy bottle-base glasses that made his eyes look small and very round and had a pencil moustache that made him look like a fascist dictator.

On his right was a police sergeant with a ponytail and a notepad where she was writing down everything he was saying. Right then she was waiting, watching him. She glanced up at me as I came in and said, "Good afternoon, Detective."

Abdo Deng opened his eyes to look at me, and the man on his

left said, "I am Kingsley Abubakar. I am Mr. Deng's attorney, and I am representing him here. Please address everything through me."

I glanced at him but didn't pay him much more attention than that. I jerked my chin at Abdo and asked him, "Are you confessing to the murder of Ana Orcera?"

He gave a feeble nod and said, "Yeah, I kill her."

"For what reason?"

He sighed, groaned, and closed his eyes. "I already explain this. Read cute cop's notes."

Cute cop didn't wait to be asked.

"He said, 'She was driving me crazy, always some group or course or studying something, and always out in the street, never at home where a woman belongs. I warn her she betta get used to being with a real Muslim man who expect a woman to be a real woman. Or she gonna find out what punishment is all about . . .' Should I continue, Detective?"

"No," I growled. "I've heard enough." I grabbed a straight-backed chair from the wall and set it beside Abdo. "So you killed her because she was a disobedient woman."

"It's what I said."

"So why did you kill her that way? Couldn't you just have stabbed her, the way you killed all the rest of your victims?"

He opened his eyes. His breathing was labored and rasped in his throat.

"You driving me crazy with your questions. I offer to cooperate, to offer you help in your fight against the crime, but all you doin' is torture me and make it seem like I am liar and cheat. I am tellin' truth!"

"Great, I am glad to hear it. Now how about you tell me why you killed her that way?"

"I don't know. She make me crazy. I beat her, I hit her. She fall on the floor, and her crying and moaning make me more crazy, and I kick her and kick her again. She all the time begging, 'Please, Abbo, not hurt me, please.' Make me sick. So I kill her."

"What about the music, Abdo?"

"Fuckin' Christian music. She is always, 'Now I am a Christian, now I am going to Islam, now I am Buddha, now I am angel from other planet.' I say, 'You born fuckin' Christian whore. Now you gonna die fuckin' Christian whore!'"

"Who chose it?"

He frowned at me. "I don't remember."

"Come on! It sure as hell wasn't in her music collection. And I know for sure it wasn't in yours. So you must have bought it."

He shrugged. "Yeah, maybe I buy it. Yeah, yeah, I buy it. Okay, I remember."

"So you knew you were going to kill her."

He looked at me sullenly, but he didn't answer. I leaned forward. "It was her death music, right? You chose it especially for her." I glanced over at his attorney. He was completely impassive with his small, round, magnified eyes. "So you bought it as part of her killing. You *knew* you were going to kill her."

"Yeah, man, you tell me. Whatever you say, that is the truth."

I leaned back. "So tell me about Cavendish, then."

"What you want me to tell you?"

Dehan suddenly snapped. "Hey, pal! You called us here. You said you wanted to confess. So here we are."

"I am weak. I just be operated. You shot me."

I glanced at Dehan, but she was avoiding my eye. I spoke to Abdo. "Nobody forced you to have this meeting, Abdo. Why did you call us here if you don't want to talk?"

"Everybody accusin' me of things. When I was in surgery, I knew I was going to die, and God come to me and say, talk to police detectives, tell them you are guilty, or you can never go to heaven. And I can feel you pressing your finger in my wound, covering my mouth with water, screaming at me, 'You are guilty! You are guilty!' And I know I must make peace with my God, *Allahu Akbar!*"

"I'm still waiting for you to tell me why you killed Mathew Cavendish."

"He was enemy of God, *Allahu Akbar.*"

"What made him an enemy of God, Abdo?"

"Please, stop torturing me. He was enemy of God. I am Jihad. He must die. Saul Arender, Jew pig, enemy of God. He must die. Judge Jones, refuse in my taxi . . ."

"You took him in your taxi?"

"Yeah, I take, in my taxi. I give him chance. I say, 'You are good judge, strong, you can join Islam.' He say me, 'No, Islam is stupid religion, I am Christian!' So he must die too."

"Georgina Cheng? Reginald Jensen?"

"Enemies of God, come in my taxi, I offer them light of God, but they say no, Islam is stupid religion. I am Jihad, I must kill."

"You offer everyone who gets in your taxi the chance to become a Muslim?"

"Yes, yes, anything you tell me is truth. Just stop torturing me. Stop to make me suffer. Please. I say anything you want."

"I'm nearly done, Abdo, and nobody is torturing you here. We are here because you invited us to hear your confession. So tell me this. What were you doing at the warehouse where we found you?"

"I have to leave my apartment. My boss tell me I must finish my job. I have nowhere to work and nowhere to live. My friend say me, 'You come and stay in my warehouse. You can live good there until you finding new place to work and live.'"

"Why were you shooting at the cops when we found you?"

"You save me. When cops come, my friends say me, you have to shoot at cops, or we kill you. You come then and shoot them, thank you, thank you, Allah will be merciful with you, because you save me then, and I can escape. They kill me if I don't shoot. They are bad men. I don't know they are bad, then they say me, 'You must kill police!' I am like, 'No, no, I no kill police!' 'If . . .'" He paused like he was becoming distressed. "'If you no kill police, we kill you!' So I must shoot, but always I shoot to miss."

"Yeah?" I laughed out loud. "And what about the prostitutes, Abdo? And what about the contracts to kill?"

He was shaking his head. "No, no, I no kill nobody. I no hurt nobody."

"Except the six people you killed when you bought them music: Reginald Jensen, Georgina Cheng, Judge Jones, Saul Arender, Mathew Cavendish, and Ana Orcera. Those you did kill, right?"

"You make me confuse. I crazy."

"Answer the damn question and stop playacting, Abdo!"

"Okay! Okay! Yes, I kill them!"

"And you used your taxi to connect with the people, that's how you offered them the chance to convert to Islam?"

"Yes! Is what I say! Yes. I use my taxi. I offer word of God. They say no. I kill!"

And you started doing this after you killed Ana, six years ago?"

"Yes, yes, please stop torture. I confess, yes."

I stood and put the chair back against the wall. "Sergeant?" Ponytail looked up at me. "That will be fine. Go back to the station, type up your notes, and leave your report on my desk."

"Yes, Detective."

She rose and left the room. I jerked my head at Dehan and stepped out into the corridor. She came with me. Outside I told her, "We don't touch him, we don't talk to him, we don't go near him until he is fully recovered. Any interviews we have with him are to be videoed. We don't address a word to him that is not on film."

She sighed and looked down at her boots. "I hear you."

"Now, let's go somewhere. I need a large whiskey, and we need to talk."

FIFTEEN

I TOOK A COUPLE OF STEPS TOWARD THE ELEVATORS then stopped and turned back. My cell rang, and I answered it. I listened for thirty seconds and said, "You are absolutely certain about that?"

The voice on the other end said they were. I thanked them and hung up.

I placed my finger gently on her collarbone.

"Abdo and his attorney don't know that we have Abdul Abbas and Farouk Bahjat?"

"No."

"Good. We need to break them yesterday, before we have to hand them over to the Feds, and get them to give us Abdo. We interrogate them separately and give each of them the chance of a deal. The one who takes it first, and gives us Abdo, gets it. The other goes down."

"Right. Stone?"

"What?"

"What's on your mind?"

"Wait. Have you spoken to the DA yet?"

"About Abdo? No."

"But you've charged him."

"Not yet. Stone, you've gone off half-cocked. I'm sorry, I don't want you balling me out again about how you've got thirty years' experience. I trust you implicitly, but I don't know what you're doing. The whole process of this operation, he *asked* to confess . . . Where were you? Where have you been?"

"Yeah, I know. Don't charge him yet. Hold off as long as you can. When you charge him, if I am not there, charge him with the offenses at the warehouse. We can always expand it. I do not want him charged with the six music murders."

"You're talking like you're going somewhere. What the hell's going on, Stone?"

I looked at her for a long moment. "He's not the guy."

"He's confessed, Stone."

"And his freaky attorney in there"—I pointed back at the room—"who looks like his folks share the family neuron on a rotating basis, is going to stand up in court and show just how smart he really is as he tears that confession to shreds. He accuses us of torture twice directly and several more times indirectly. And however justified the shooting was, he is going to use it as one more example of police brutality. That confession is not worth a damn."

"Come on, Stone! Why bother confessing in the first place? All he needs to do is allege brutality from the start."

I shook my head. "That wouldn't stick. But a confession in which he begs for us to stop torturing him will muddy the water and confuse the jury. Plus, he knows we can't pin those six murders on him, so he pleads guilty, then alleges we forced a confession out of him, and the chances are high that he'll be acquitted, not just of the six he didn't commit, but all the ones he did commit too. Our case will not be proven beyond a reasonable doubt, will it? It's a smart move, and further evidence that his attorney is not as stupid as he looks."

She was shaking her head. "That is a long reach, Stone. Too long."

"Yeah, I know, but Abdo as the music killer leaves too many

things unexplained. And one of those unexplained things is, why the hell is he confessing to six murders he has absolutely no reason to confess to? Do you believe Allah came down and spoke to him? Because I don't. So what made him confess?"

She didn't answer. She just stood looking up at me.

I shrugged. "I need to think about what I do next. I think I know who did this, and I think I know why. All I am asking is you hold off on charging Abdo with the six music killings until you have enough evidence. But for God's sake charge him with the stuff you can make stick right away."

She was frowning hard and shook her head. "What are you saying? You don't want me as your partner anymore?"

"No, I am not saying that, for crying out loud! But you think I've lost my grip on the case and I am dreaming up scenarios that fit with some crazy interest in philosophy. So, if I mess up badly, you can always step back and say, 'I was not part of that. Stone went crazy all on his own.'"

"I should slap your face for that. When have I ever been disloyal to you?"

"Never, but you think I am chasing rainbows in this case. So I am giving you the option to pursue the case you believe in instead of the one you don't. Personally I think you're nuts, and the fact that he is *not* guilty of these murders stands out like a neon dildo at the vicar's tea party. But hey, I only have thirty years' experience, so don't listen to me."

I grinned to show I was only half serious. She sighed and shook her head.

"You can be a real asshole sometimes, Stone. Did you know that? Now you listen to me. We are partners, and as long as we remain partners, we are going to investigate this case together, not as rivals, but as partners. And if two lines of evidence emerge, then we are going to explore them both, together. You want to work alone, I think that is real sad, because I think we make a good team. But you go ahead and talk to the inspector. You want us to continue as a team, you stop making up excuses to cut me out."

"No." I suppressed the small knot of panic. "I do not want to work alone. But I do want you to listen to what I have to say instead of attributing it to a fanciful desire to tackle philosophical cases. Can we get back to the investigation now?"

"Please."

"Abdo Deng is not the guy. His confession is false, and I can prove it to you."

"How?"

"In two ways. The second of those ways will be introducing you to the real killer. The first is conveying to you the content of my conversation with the TLC."

"You conversed with Tender Loving Care?"

"The New York City Taxi and Limousine Commission."

"Oh, what was the content of your conversation with them?"

"That Abdo Deng has been driving a New York taxicab for just three years. So he could not have made contact with Mathew Cavendish or Saul Arender in his taxi. His whole confession is a crock of horse manure."

She sighed heavily, turned away, and rubbed her face with her hands.

"*Shit!*" She turned back to me, her hands open, and looking up at the ceiling like she expected to see Jehovah there and have words with him. "Why didn't I check that?"

"Because he fit the bill of who you expected the killer to be, Dehan."

"Yeah, thanks. Don't pull your punches on my account."

"Like it or not, this killer is a person who is obsessed with . . ." My brain stalled. Dehan watched me, waiting for the word.

"Obsessed with what?"

"I want to say redemption, but that's not it."

"With salvation? With saving souls?"

I nodded. "Something like that. He sees his victims as lost souls. He thinks he knows where they have gone wrong, and he tries to set them on the right path."

"Their death is their salvation."

"Yes." I nodded again. "Yes, that's right. Their death is their salvation."

We stared at each other a moment, suddenly aware that that fact had meaning. My cell rang, startlingly loud in the quiet corridor. I answered.

"Yeah, Stone."

"Detective, this is Javi Dominguez. You had me looking into the backgrounds of the victims . . ."

"Yeah, I remember, Javi. What have you got?"

"Well, it may be nothing, Detective Stone, but I thought I should mention it just in case . . ."

"What is it?"

"I knew we were having trouble finding a connection between the victims, so I thought it might be a good idea to look into the financial activities of the victims and their families and cross-reference them."

"That's very good, Dominguez. What did you find?"

I put it on speaker, and Dehan came up close.

"I was pretty surprised, Detective Stone. It was Judge Jeremiah Jones' wife, back in December 2014, she donated twenty thousand bucks to Reverend Morton's mission. That was about a year after he was sacked from the St. George, and he was reinventing himself as an independent preacher, and one and a half years before the first victim."

"Did they stay in contact after that?"

"That's kind of hard to tell, and I wanted to talk to you before approaching her direct. But I did find there were further, smaller donations over the next few years. We'd have to request records the last two years, but from the records solicited by Detective Epstein, it looks like she was a regular contributor to the, uh . . . Church of Divine Grace and Rebirth. Another thing that surprised me, Detective Stone . . ."

"Yeah?"

"Well, how come Detective Epstein didn't notice that?"

"I guess he was looking in the wrong place. This is very good work, Dominguez, and it's the right way to investigate. Keep exploring along those lines and keep me posted."

I hung up. Dehan had her left eye closed and was repressing a smile. I said, "What?"

"Penny O'Connor this, Penny O'Connor that, I want Penny O'Connor to do it because she's more lively . . .'"

"Haven't you got some sinners to barbeque with your pitchfork, Dehan?"

"Oh, that's very nice, coming from a godless WASP. Who do you want to talk to, Mrs. Hanging Judge or Mr. Fire and Brimstone?"

I rubbed my chin and cheek. It felt and sounded like sandpaper. "I don't know," I muttered.

"There goes another idol. I thought you knew everything."

"Reverend Morton Wells. I want to talk to Reverend Morton Wells. And I hope you're not expecting to sleep tonight."

I turned and pressed the Down button on the elevator.

"Why?" She was frowning. "I thought we had Dominguez and *Penny O'Connor* doing our research for us."

"Not research." I shook my head. The doors slid open, and we stepped in. She was still frowning.

"What then?"

"As soon as we get home, I plan to tan your hide so hard you won't be able to sit down for a week."

Her eyebrows crawled all the way up to her hairline. "I'd like to see you try!"

"Well you just hold my beer and see if I don't."

"Jerk!"

As the doors slid open on the ground floor, I reprimanded her. "Talk right, for God's sake, Dehan. You're a New Yorker, from the Bronx. It's 'joik'! 'Joik' like that. 'Joik.'"

"Does it help you think when you do this, Stone? Tell me there is a reason."

"It does." I turned to face her and held her shoulders in my hands. "How many victims can we link the reverend to?"

She was shaking her head and making an expression like I was giving her wind.

"No, Stone, no. No way."

"Fine, I'm sure you're right, and if you are, you have nothing to worry about. How many people?"

"So far? Ana Orcera and Judge Jones. That's it."

"But there is at least an even chance that anyone who was close to Judge Jones might have had contact with Saul Arender."

"I guess." She didn't sound real enthusiastic.

I turned and propelled her gently toward the exit.

"Remind me, what was the central premise, for want of a better word, of Morton Wells' philosophy?"

She puffed out her cheeks and looked up at the ceiling. People jostled past us. She intoned a semi-chant. "He chuckled and asked if I was Jewish, said he liked the Jewish view of sin. It was more understanding of, uh . . . the human condition, and more forgiving. I think forgiveness was the big thing. He said Catholics got stuck in the Old Testament. They were forever trying to forget Jesus and what he said about forgiveness. And he said that instead, they used him to make people feel guilty. Then he said God was omnipresent and omnipotent. I remember he said that He was literally—not figuratively, *literally*—everywhere, and that He was literally able to do *absolutely* everything and anything. What else? He said that you only needed to think for a fraction of a second to see that all people needed so they could achieve forgiveness from God was to know themselves, *understand* themselves and their fallibility as humans, and then *forgive* themselves. His—God's—forgiveness was implicit in their own forgiveness, *because* He is omnipotent. And finally, at the end, he said he hoped that as Ana lay bleeding to death and unable to move, she forgave herself *and* her killer, for allowing such a terrible thing to happen."

"That's very impressive, Dehan, but in one word?"

"Forgiveness."

"Which is not a million light years from salvation."

She made a noise like "djah!" and started walking toward the exit, adding, "At a stretch."

I followed and pushed the door open for her to go through, out into the parking lot. "Not such a stretch, Dehan, if you happen to be a Christian. To a committed Christian, God's forgiveness and salvation are one and the same thing. But, as you pointed out not five minutes ago, in Reverend Wells' view, we achieve God's forgiveness by forgiving ourselves. Am I right?"

She nodded, heading for the car. "Yeah, for a change." She walked on, then stopped and turned to face me. She looked mad and defeated. "And you think he believes that these poor bastards have forgiven themselves thanks to the bizarre deaths he has arranged for them."

The Jag was parked in the shade of a copse of London plane trees. She turned and walked to it, and when she got there she climbed on the hood and sat looking at me. I sat opposite her, on the lawn.

"The question for us now, Dehan," I said, "is not his motivation or how crazy he is. What we need to be looking at is how we prove that it's him. And we need to start by connecting each of the victims to him. How do we do that?"

She took a deep breath and stared up into the foliage. "I'll go along with you, Stone, but I think you're wrong. Okay, it all starts with Ana Orcera."

"Yes."

"And Abdo Deng . . ."

I shook my head. "No, it starts with Ana Orcera and her laziness."

"Her *laziness?* Are you kidding me?"

"No. It was her laziness that led her to neglect her son, that led her to allow Abdo Deng into her life, that led her to try one quick-fix cult or religion after another—and to abandon each one before really trying. Her laziness, or sloth, was her mortal sin, and it is that which gets her killed."

"Okay, let me think this through. Reverend Morton Wells

takes a shine to Ana, who is part of his congregation. He likes her, maybe even starts to become infatuated with her. He can see she is lazy, indolent, slothful, and he decides to make her a special project, and tries to set her on the right path. One thing leads to another, and Abdo Deng appears on the scene, a parasite living off her and abusing her and her son. He tries to persuade her to dump him, but instead she dumps the reverend and, adding insult to injury, returns to the Catholic Church. Reverend Morton Wells goes over the edge and kills her."

"How?"

"He breaks her arms and legs. That is both an expression of his own rage and frustration and, in his mind, a way of making her think about her own paralysis as her life ebbs away when he stabs her. How am I doing?"

"You're doing fine. So what happens next?"

"Next? Next his craziness gets out of hand, and the only way he can come to terms with what he has done is by convincing himself that he is doing God's work."

SIXTEEN

I GRUNTED, AND WE STARED AT EACH OTHER FOR A while. I pulled a blade of grass and examined it.

"Okay, so how do we move from Ana Orcera to Mathew Cavendish?"

She shook her head and shrugged. "There's what Epstein told us. They were at Drew University together, and they were both part of the debating club. They debated against each other, Epstein said in and out of the club."

I nodded. "There is another possible connection. Something Dominguez mentioned to me. Cavendish published some articles in a couple of magazines: *The Free Thinker*, which is a successful online magazine and forum for debate, and the *Philosopher's Monthly*, which is a venerable old glossy. He was also invited to talk at the Ingersoll Institute, which is an institute that promotes free thinking and atheism. The point is, the impression I got from Reverend Morton Wells was that he was something of an intellectual and the kind of man who might keep abreast of thinking in that kind of area, even if just to refute it."

"Yeah, and thinking back to what Epstein told us at the beginning, he had mentioned Arender in some of his sermons. Maybe, Stone, what we are looking at here is a guy who is slowly being consumed by . . ." I waited; she stared at me, then narrowed her eyes and intoned the word as a question: "*Guilt?*"

I grunted. "That's interesting, Dehan."

"Okay, I am going to take a little walk on the wild side here, Stone, just bear with me. He is a Christian, and like all the children of Abraham, guilt is hardwired into his psyche. But for him it is worse, because he has impure thoughts and feelings toward people he shouldn't oughtta. To his enduring shame, he is accused by the kids at St. George's and is never able to clear his name. And that eats at him, along with the guilt he feels. With time, he becomes obsessed with the idea of helping and redeeming lost souls, but what he is really trying to do is redeem himself, and purge himself of his appetites and desires. But because he cannot face his own self-loathing and disgust, he starts to project it onto people who, for one reason or another, are important to him. First the woman he is infatuated with, and next his old rival, Mathew Cavendish."

I frowned. "Have you been reading Freud?"

She smiled on one side of her face but left her eyes out of the operation. "Yeah, I heard it was all about sex, but actually it's quite tame."

"Fine, what about the way he was killed, with all those elaborate ropes?"

She pulled up her knees and hugged them, and rested her chin on them.

"The ropes were . . . redundant?" I nodded. "Excessive, unnecessary . . ."

I smiled. "Did you happen to know, Dehan, that in Aramaic . . ."

"That's the language they spoke in the Bible."

"It's the language Jesus spoke; in Aramaic, the word for camel is the same as the word for rope, *gml*."

"You're kidding me."

"Not at all."

"So it's easier to thread a rope through the eye of a needle than for a rich man to go to heaven. But all you need to do is strip away the excess, until only the essential is left."

"I begin to feel we are onto something, Dehan."

"And the point is labored because of what he is tied to, the heaviest and most valuable of his furniture."

I wagged a finger at her. "But here it becomes interesting, because suddenly the music changes. We have a clear, powerful biblical reference, but the music is Japanese Zen music."

"Epstein described it as jerky and weird."

"Yeah, the idea of Zen is to try and kind of trip you up into seeing reality as it is in the now. Zen is all about being, here and now. So, in the now there are no processes, right? Everything just is."

She was frowning and arching an eyebrow at the same time. "Okay, I think . . ."

"So in Zen music they will often develop a phrase and break it at exactly the wrong time, or interrupt it in a jarring way, to bring the listener into the now. It's what a Zen master will do to his student: jar him awake."

"So here was Cavendish, his old rival, tied to his wealth and his possessions . . ."

"More than that," I interrupted, "tied to materialism. Remember he was the atheist, the empiricist, who turned to Buddhism. You recall Cavendish was gassed? I wonder if that gas was supposed to ignite with the spark from the music center. The ultimate awakening shock."

She snorted. "Good morning, dear, here's your coffee, *boom*!"

"Graphic as ever. So next we have Saul Arender . . ."

"And we know from Epstein that the reverend was aware of him as an attorney and actively disapproved of his work."

"We'll need to confirm it, but that shouldn't be too difficult. As I recall, Epstein said he mentioned Arender in a few sermons and described him as a criminal attorney, a Jew, and a servant of Satan. What is interesting here, Dehan, is that we are seeing connections between these people and the reverend that are not the product of something artificial, like a taxi, but a direct consequence of his way of life. What brings these people together is actually *him*."

She nodded, a little impatient. "Yeah, so, his death. He was hanged with a piano wire and an elaborate system whereby the harder he tried to break free, the tighter the noose became, until finally it decapitated him."

I picked a blade of grass and stared at it. "Decapitated . . ."

"Killed by his own efforts to get free . . ."

"Piano wire . . ."

"I don't see it, Stone."

I tried a new approach. "He is an advocate for evil, for the Devil, as the reverend said."

She nodded. "Okay . . ."

"He devotes his life to trying to set other people free . . ."

"Okay, that's good, and his efforts to set evil people free must lead in the end to his own destruction . . . ?"

I spread my hands. "Nobody said they had to be masterpieces of symbolic representation. It hangs together, even if it's not as neat as Cavendish's ropes."

"Which brings us to Three Jay, Judge Jeremiah Jones." She pointed at me like her hand was a gun and she was going to shoot me. "Now, we know from what Dominguez discovered that *Mrs.* Jeremiah Jones knew *of* Reverend Wells, and we have to assume that, having made such a generous donation, she didn't just know *of* him, but actually knew him, personally, and she must have known him for some time. So, we have Saul Arender on the one hand, who is a close friend of the judge, and you have the judge on the other side, whose wife is very much aware of the reverend. It is almost impossible that the reverend was not aware of the judge."

I nodded. "I agree, especially as the reverend was taking enough of an interest in Arender's cases to accuse him of being the Devil's advocate, and we know for a fact that Arender frequently came before Judge Jones. He must have been aware of his judgments and his sentences."

"Something we'll have to prove. Maybe Mrs. Judge Jones can confirm it for us. So what about his death?"

I flicked the blade of grass into the breeze.

"He was impaled with a decorative sword he had hanging in his office. He was tied up on the floor, and the sword was suspended from a rope just above his chest. Just beneath the rope, on a small occasional table, there was a candle that was slowly burning through the rope. He could see this happening and had to simply accept and await his death. The music selected for him was Gregorian chants."

She pulled down the corners of her mouth. "So, 'Judge not, lest ye be judged.'" Now she wagged a finger at me. "But there is more."

"Tell me."

"He is forced to feel and understand the despair of a person trapped in a relentless, pitiless system. I don't mean just the criminal justice system, but in a society that has no room for the weak, for lost souls as he calls them, but destroys them as people—as souls, Stone—it traps them and destroys them, and they cannot escape."

I thought about it for a moment. "It's a subtle take on the sword of Damocles."

She rolled her eyes. "Yeah, I thought that too."

"Damocles was a courtier at the court of King Dionysius. He was always telling Dionysius how lucky he was to be so powerful. So the king told Damocles he would swap places with him for a day. Damocles agreed and prepared himself to spend a day enjoying all the wealth and power of the king. What he overlooked was that Dionysius had been very cruel and made a lot of enemies in his rise to power, and to convey this to Damocles, he had a sword suspended over the throne hanging from its pommel on a single horsehair. So as long as Damocles sat on the throne, he had to be constantly aware of the imminent threat of death. This was the aspect of power that Damocles had overlooked. Those who exercise power become targets, and the more power they wield, the more at risk they are."

She was quiet for a bit, looking up into the boughs of the plane trees. Eventually she said, "But Damocles always had the option of stepping down and handing the power back to the king."

I smiled. "That may have been the killer's point. Because though Damocles had that option, for Dionysius it was almost impossible, and the deeper you get into the systems of power, the more difficult it is to escape, until in the end it destroys you."

"Gregorian chants," she said, absently. "He was an evangelist."

"Preaching for a church that had hurt Reverend Wells very badly."

She took a deep breath. "That's four out of six. It leaves us with Georgina Cheng and Reginald Jensen."

"Georgina Cheng we know he was aware of because he attacked her in his sermons. Again, we need to confirm it, and Epstein can tell us where he got that information. Her death was clearly simply a case of making her aware of how the animals she vivisected felt. She was fed curare and had her limbs amputated. Then she was left to die, listening to sacred Tudor music."

She pursed her lips and made a face of skepticism. "Gotta say, it doesn't scream 'Christian guilt' at me."

"No, it's an odd choice. She is always the odd one out."

"It all makes sense except the music. Why wouldn't he select Buddhist monks chanting 'Om' or something?" She paused and looked at me. "We are back to that again."

I shrugged. "We should ask him."

She grunted softly. "Before we do, what about Reginald Jensen?"

"Schrödinger's cat. This has been troubling me from the very start. With all the others I can see how a person—a self-elected judge—could judge them and find them wanting and set them a punishment that fits the crime with the intention that in death they should be redeemed. But Reginald Jensen? His crime was what? To love his cat? And the music, the man is a Buddhist, the only one out of the six who was an actual Buddhist, and the music is sacred Renaissance . . .”

I stopped, and it seemed to me for a moment that the whole of New York had stopped. There was a fraction of a fraction of a second, a moment so small it could not be measured and slipped into infinity, in which I had complete clarity. I saw the whole crime as it was, in all its perfection and its execution, its motive and its purpose. For a moment too small to measure, there was absolute stillness, and then the leaves overhead rustled again, a bird sang, like the very first bird singing for the very first time, a breeze touched my face, and a car sighed past on Seminole Avenue. Dehan blinked once, slowly, and asked, “You okay?”

I nodded. “Yeah, it was all in the music.”

“It was?”

“Yeah. Renaissance. It was a time when a lot changed in Europe, not least the music, and the religion it represented.”

“You’re going to have to explain that, Stone. Miles Davis is about as far out as I get.”

“I’m not sure I can. I need to think it through before I can put it into words.” I thought a moment, chewing my lip. “Thomas More, a man trapped by the Renaissance and the English Reformation, between Catholicism and the new ideas that were flooding Europe at the time, wrote a lament at the death of Queen Elizabeth. It went: ‘O! Ye that put your trust and confidence in worldly joy and frail prosperity, that so live here as ye should never hence, remember death and look here upon me.’”

“Kind of guy everyone wants to invite to their party.”

“Death and rebirth, Dehan. That’s what it’s all about, death and rebirth.”

“So how do we prove it?”

I stood and wiped the grass and dirt from my ass with my hands.

"Well, first of all we need to go and talk to Reverend Morton Wells again and see what he has to say for himself. Then we need to place our killer at the scene of every crime."

She watched me from the hood of the Jag. "Oh, is that all? I thought it might be something difficult that involved police work."

"Not this time, Dehan. This time, the mountain is going to come to Mohamed."

"And the religious allusions just keep coming."

"And that"—I held out my hand, and she took it, before sliding off the car—"is where we have been going wrong."

"It is? Come on, Stone. You know it drives me crazy when you do this. Talk straight."

"This whole case, from Ana Orcera all the way to Reginald Jensen, we have assumed it was about religion and redemption. It is not. It is about . . ."

I paused and pulled open the door. Dehan sighed and went around to the passenger side. "What, Stone? It's about what?"

I looked at her across the roof, her face touched by the failing, dappled light. "I am trying to think of the plural for phoenix."

"There is only one Phoenix, Stone. It's in Arizona."

"Phoenices. This case is about phoenices: souls reborn from the hell of their own deaths."

"You're taking me way out of my depth, Stone. Isn't that redemption? Being reborn from your own hell?"

"Redemption is being forgiven by God. Serving in heaven. Rebirth is re-creating yourself from your own ashes, reshaping your own soul from your own spiritual suffering. Rather than serving in heaven, it's ruling in hell."

She shook her head. "I sure hope you know what the hell you're talking about, Stone. Because I sure as hell don't!"

SEVENTEEN

I SAT BEHIND THE WHEEL OF THE JAG AND CALLED THE
Reverend Morton Wells. I had the door open, and I could hear
the birds chattering in the trees above me. It rang six times and
went to his answering service. I looked at my watch. It was almost
seven p.m. I called the church. It rang twice, and a woman
answered.

"Hello?" Before I could answer, she said, "You're lucky to
catch me. I am usually home by now. How can I help you? The
reverend is not in . . ."

I interrupted her. "This is Detective Stone, of the New York
Police Department. Who am I speaking to?"

"Oh, I am Mrs. Howard, Reverend Wells' secretary, assistant,
and general factotum!" She gave a coy laugh. "I am usually all
done by now and back at home providing the same service for my
husband!"

"And I am sure you do a fine job, Mrs. Howard. The thing is,
I need to speak to the reverend fairly urgently. Can you tell me
where I can find him?"

"Well, yes, one of our benefactors called and asked him to go
and visit . . ."

"Who was that benefactor, Mrs. Howard?"

"Well, I suppose it's all right. You *are* the police, after all. It was Mrs. Jones, the judge's widow. She called a couple of hours ago and asked for the reverend to go and see her. I mean, she *is* a generous contributor, but it *is* rather an imposition, to ask a busy man to drop everything and . . ."

"Where is Mrs. Jones, Mrs. Howard? Is she in New York City, or . . . ?"

"Oh, no!" There was no hiding the scorn in her voice. "No, she is at their country house in Dutchess County, Chelsea. The great lady summons and he must drop everything and go. I'm sorry if I am uncharitable, but I believe in calling them as I see them."

"Have you got an address, Mrs. Howard? I've tried his cell, and he isn't answering."

There was a small sigh, then, "Yes, just hold the line . . ."

There were a few thumps, the sound of drawers being opened and closed, then a loud rustle, and her voice came back to the telephone.

"It's on River Road South, right on the river, eight bedrooms, huge lawn, not that I have ever been invited, but I've seen pictures."

She gave me the number, and after a little grumble she hung up, and I sat looking at Dehan.

"She called a couple of hours ago. It's an hour and a half's drive there, so he'll stay for dinner. Is he going to drive back after a fine claret and half a bottle of port or a couple of fine whiskeys? I don't think so. He'll stay the night."

"So the question is, do we go and spoil the party?"

"And the answer is, clearly, yes. We do."

We took the Pelham Parkway west and joined the Bronx River Parkway at the Bronx Park interchange. Then it was pretty much a straight drive north through Westchester and Putnam until we came to Shenandoah, and there we turned west onto the I-84 and finally came off at Glenham, onto the NY 52, and Red Schoolhouse Road, where things started to get quaint. It was after eight o'clock and getting dark, but as we turned finally onto River Road South and started weaving among copses and sweeping lawns and tiny roads called things like Heather Drive and Woodcrest Court, we knew we were a lot more than an hour and a half from the Bronx.

At eight thirty we pulled off River Road South and cruised up two hundred yards of gravel drive to a large house set among fir trees, with at least four gabled roofs and half a dozen tall chimney pots, two of which were trailing woodsmoke into the evening air. The windows beneath the gables were leaded in a rhomboid pattern with warm amber light leeching through them, and there was abundant ivy crawling up the redbrick walls.

The drive ended in a flat, asphalt parking area with a round, silent fountain at the center. Three broad, shallow steps led up to a large porch and a heavy oak door. Two lamps flanked the door and illuminated it. It was somewhere between chocolate box and Christmas card, only a lot more expensive.

We stepped up to the door and rang the bell. It must have rung deep inside the house, because we didn't hear it. So after a couple of minutes we rang again.

Dehan said, "I don't see a car." I nodded. She shrugged. "It might be in a parking garage."

"Maybe."

She walked away, down the side of the house. She left the asphalt, and I heard her boots crunch on the gravel as she slowly disappeared from view. I went round back, following an asphalt path that led to a couple of garages. The blinds were rolled down, and there was no way to peer through, but I figured they could fit at least four cars in there. One of them might be the reverend's.

I heard Dehan calling and went back the way I had come, then followed her gravel path till I came to a picket fence with a gate. On the other side was a patio and a large swimming pool, a couple of tables with parasols, and half a dozen chairs. There were some sliding glass doors onto the patio, but the drapes were drawn closed, and no sound came from within.

Dehan was standing back, looking up at a couple of windows with light seeping through. One of the windows was slightly open. She called again, and I went and hammered on the plate glass. Nothing happened.

I went and joined Dehan, who was dialing a number on her phone. We stood in silence while it rang. She said, "They've gone out for dinner or they're in postcoital stupor."

"Wow..." I frowned. "Wait, stay very still and very quiet..."

We stood motionless in the dark, with only the limpid amber glow from the windows touching the closed parasols and reflecting on the water in the pool. The only sounds were the lapping of small waves and the creek of a woodcock. Then Dehan touched my arm.

"There..."

And there it was again, a high-pitched sound, not quite a wail, sustained.

I swore violently, pulled my semiautomatic from my holster, and ran for the sliding glass doors. Dehan was right behind me, her pistol in her hands. I didn't pause. I put two rounds through the glass. It shattered and fell in a glittering, lethal cascade. I kicked out the few shards that were left and stepped into a large, dark drawing room. It was gloomy, with deep shadows in the corners. Dehan pushed me away from the window into the shadows, so I'd stop making a silhouette, and moved to her right.

I hunkered down and took out the pen flashlight I keep in my pocket. Dehan had done the same, and the thin beams played around the room. There was nothing to see but heavy, old-fashioned furniture and English hunting prints on the walls.

I crossed to the door and flipped on the lights.

I said, "Upstairs," and yanked open the door into a large, oak-paneled hall in a pseudo-baronial style. There was a heavy mahogany staircase rising up the far side of the hall, and I ran, taking the steps two at a time. Dehan snapped on the light on the landing. I had a rough idea in my head that the room with the lights would be on the right, but now I heard the music clearly. It seemed to be late Medieval sacred choral music.

Dehan passed me at a sprint, rounded a corner, and we came to a large oak door. It was locked, and she blew out the lock and kicked open the door. Mrs. Jones was there. She was suspended by her ankles from one of the crossbeams of her vast, four-poster bed. Her wrists were tied behind her back, and her head was inside a large, silver ice bucket. But it wasn't filled with ice at that moment—it was filled with champagne that was being fed in via a short hose from a vast bottle on her bedside table.

I didn't pause. I kicked the bucket from under her head, spilling its golden, fizzing contents on the Persian rug, while Dehan hacked at the rope with her pocketknife. She fell to the floor, and I rolled her on her back. She had no pulse, and she was not breathing. While Dehan called it in, I started CPR. But I knew before I started that it was too late. She was gone, and all the while the Renaissance choir chanted at us: "O! Ye that put your trust and confidence in worldly joy and frail prosperity, that so live here as ye should never hence, remember death and look here upon me!"

Eventually I stopped. I stopped kissing death, while her swollen face goggled at the ceiling above me, and her swollen tongue lolled in her mouth. I stood and walked to the door. Dehan came with me and put a hand on my shoulder.

"She was gone. There was nothing you could do."

I looked at her. "Why so soon?"

She frowned. "What?"

"For six years it has been one a year. Now suddenly a new victim within days."

"Because he knows we are about to close in on him."

"Abdo Deng is in the hospital. There is no way he could do this in his condition, even if he discharged himself. Hoisting her with that rope requires real strength."

"The reverend was working out when we went to see him."

I nodded. "We need to go."

"The sheriff is on his way."

"The sheriff will have to wait." I handed her the keys. "Give me the phone."

I called him as we ran down the stairs.

"This is Sheriff Adrianson . . ."

"This is Detective John Stone, NYPD Forty-Third Precinct. I am calling to tell you we are leaving the scene of the crime at River Road South." I reached the bottom of the stairs and sprinted for the door. "Judge Jeremiah Jones' widow's house . . ."

"Now you look here, young man, you will stay put until . . ."

"I am really not that young, Sheriff, and I have at least one imminent murder to prevent tonight, so you'll have to forgive me. We'll talk tomorrow!"

"Now you . . . !"

I didn't hear the rest because I hung up, and Dehan made the old Jag snarl and jump before I had closed the door.

"Where?" she said.

"The Church of Divine Grace and Rebirth, and you had better make this thing fly!" I was calling the 43rd as I spoke. "Inspector, I have powerful reasons to believe that there is a murder in progress at the Church of Divine Grace and Rebirth . . ."

"But I understood you were in Dutchess County at . . ."

"I was, and now I am breaking the speed limit to get back to the Bronx; this is in the hands of the sheriff here. It is too complicated to explain over the phone, and while we argue, somebody is probably being subjected to a slow, cruel murder. You need to get a couple of patrol cars over there half an hour ago."

"Good God, John!" He sounded exasperated, but he hung up, so I figured he was contacting Dispatch.

Dehan drove fast, cutting corners through the dark lanes, the twin cones of the Jag's headlamps pushing through the mantle of darkness, picking out the twisting, arching forms of the trees and throwing their tortured black shadows against the walls of passing houses. We didn't speak. I watched her face, fine, beautiful, tense, and concentrated, with alternating dark and amber light washing across it in an urgent pulse.

Then the cat was growling, and we were surging out of the lush, green quiet of Fishkill and thundering onto the I-84 at 120 miles per hour, hurtling along the freeway toward the Taconic State Parkway.

She didn't let up, and the ancient Jaguar didn't let us down, and in little more than an hour we were slowing as we approached the end of the Bronx River Parkway, at the 43rd. We screeched and fishtailed into Story, and hit sixty before we skidded into Soundview, thundered down four blocks, and spun the Jag's ass through one hundred and eighty degrees to enter Leland Avenue, where there were two patrol cars and an ambulance sitting, waiting, doing nothing. Dehan pulled up beside one of the patrols, and we climbed out. There were four cops and two paramedics standing around, stamping their feet and talking, and the inspector was hurrying toward us from the church door, which was firmly closed.

I stepped up to him. "What's going on?"

"John." He was shaking his head. "I can't get authorization to go in. There is no probable cause, and you have given me nothing but . . ."

Hot anger welled in my gut and rose to my head. I pointed back toward Dutchess County in the north.

"Judge Jeremiah Jones' wife was drowned in champagne while listening to Renaissance music in her house in Chelsea! We just left the scene, and one very pissed sheriff, to get here!" I thrust my finger toward the church. "I am telling you there could be somebody dying in there! By now they are probably dead!"

He was scowling at me. "John, control yourself!"

"*Control myself?*"

I pushed past him and ran to the church, taking the steps three at a time. Dehan was on my heels, muttering, "Stone, what are you going to do?"

I didn't answer. I had the Sig Sauer she had made me buy in

my hand, and I blew out the lock. I heard the inspector shout my name but ignored him. I wrenched open the big, red door and blew out the lock of the smaller, wood-paneled doors behind it. I put my two hundred pounds behind a second kick, and the doors smashed open.

A long, tapering rectangle of streetlight pierced the nave. My shadow bisected it, with Dehan's just behind me. The rest was darkness, deep and impenetrable shadow that held the cavernous room engulfed. Except that at the end, where the altar stood, there was the dim, flickering light of two candles, and the heavy, sacred silence of the church was tainted with a sound that I had grown to find loathsome and disgusting: the high, almost manic voices of a choir; the pitiless, inhuman, dispassionate invocation of spiritual detachment, of light beyond compassion.

I ran down the central aisle, along the blood-red carpet, toward the altar—that altar raised to glorify death and suffering, that altar in whose name so many had died in horror and agony. There was blood, but there was no body.

The body was nailed to the cross that had been erected beyond the altar, beneath that other cross that held the eternally suffering image of the Christ. He had been nailed there, through his wrists and his ankles, and he had been pierced in his side and left to die of agonizing suffocation, listening to Guillaume Dufay, "Agnus Dei," on a loop, over and over.

Dehan stood beside me and whispered, "Jesus . . . !"

I felt a terrible grief grip like a fist at my belly and my chest. Unconsciously I recited the words I was hearing, bitter inside at their wicked irony, as behind me the church filled with those who had allowed this crime, by abiding by the law.

"Lamb of God, who takes away the sins of the world, have mercy on us. Lamb of God, who takes away the sins of the world, grant us peace . . ."

Suddenly Dehan was shouting, as though awoken from a trance.

"Get this man down! Where are the paramedics? Get them in here *now*! Get him down!"

There was a scramble of feet, voices shouting. I turned away from the horrible image of the reverend. I knew he was dead, and there was nothing anybody could do for him. I wondered if he had forgiven himself for whatever he had done in life. The inspector was standing a few feet behind me, staring up at the broken man with the blue, swollen face. I heard my own voice as though it belonged to somebody else. It was twisted, bitter.

"You could have saved him."

His eyes focused on me, frowned with incomprehension. "I tried . . ."

"You allowed this to happen. You stood at the door and refused to open it, when you knew that inside a man was in agony, dying."

"John, I . . ."

I pushed past him, past the rushing paramedics, the cops, and Dehan, and went out into the Bronx night.

EIGHTEEN

It had started to drizzle again. The meat wagon had left with its cargo of death and sacrifice, and Joe and his team of forensic scientists were working methodically from the locks which I had blown out, thus removing any evidence, to the altar and the crucifix, where no amount of 9mm rounds could ever obliterate the horror of what had happened there, of what we had been witness to.

I was sitting propped against the hood of the Jag, letting the cold, light rain cool my face. Something made me look up, and I saw Dehan's tall silhouette step out of the luminous quadrangle of the door. She stood looking at me awhile, then trotted down the steps with her hands in her leather jacket pockets. She crossed the sidewalk and stood in front of me.

"Did you know?"

I shook my head. "No, how could I have? It was an educated hunch somebody was going to get killed."

"How?"

I sighed and tried to martial my thoughts. "This killer is a mystic. That much is obvious from the murders. In all of mysticism there are two numbers that stand out above all others."

She frowned. "Why do you know that? Which ones?"

"Nine and twelve. I know that because I read a lot. The way the killings were being stacked up, one a year, it was even odds that he was aiming for a mystical number. Twelve is the number of wisdom, continuity, wealth. Nine is the number of death and rebirth, so the odds were pretty good the killer was going for nine deaths to achieve some mystical objective. We had six, but the killer was aware that we were getting close, so he might rush to reach his target early."

"Now he's at eight." I nodded. She went on, "You thought it was the reverend."

"Now the reverend is dead."

"So who's next?"

"I don't know." I stood and ran my fingers through my hair. It was sodden. I wiped my hands on my jacket, but that was wet too. "I can't get a handle on this damned thing. I think I see it and understand it, and then it turns upside down." I gestured in at the church. "He is connected to all the other victims. We established that. But how the hell does *he* become a victim? And now—right now—along with the judge's wife! She called him, told him to come and see her. Did he go? Did he ever leave New York? And how did the killer know that the reverend was going to see Mrs. Jones? Because he must have known."

"Why?"

"Because it is too much of a coincidence. We go chasing the reverend up to her house in Dutchess County only to find she has been murdered, and we come racing back to find *he* has been murdered! It's too much . . ."

I paused, feeling the cool trickles of water running down my face, down into my neck. A cold breeze rustled the leaves and sent a chill shudder down my back.

"God, Dehan, I have been so blind."

"What? What are you talking about?"

"I have been so stupid. It was staring me in the face from the very start."

"What was, Stone?"

I put my hands to my head, struggling to comprehend it. It was impossible, absurd, and yet so self-evident.

"My God," I said again. "These were mercy killings . . ."

"*What?*"

"They were mercy killings on a massive scale. Dehan, get in the car."

"You going to tell me . . ."

"No, just get in the car. Let me think."

She got in, and as I opened my own door, the figure of the inspector stepped out of the church and stood silhouetted against the light.

"John!" he called to me. "We need to talk . . ."

I shook my head. "No, sir, we don't. And I have somewhere I have to be. Let's see if I can at least save the ninth victim in this case. And sir . . . ?" I waited, but he didn't answer. "I may call you in five minutes to ask for backup or support. Do me a favor, help me out this time, will you?"

I climbed in and slammed the door. I fired up the engine, rammed in first, and floored the pedal. I did sixty down Soundview and fishtailed into Cornell, leaving a cloud of spray behind me. I skidded to a halt outside the vihara and ran down the concrete path to the door, where the two lamps illuminated the doorstep. I hammered on the wood and rang at the bell.

Dehan came up beside me and grabbed my arm. "Stone, you have to tell me what you're doing! What is happening? Where are we? Is this the Buddhist temple?"

I pulled my arm free and hammered again with my fist. "I think the last victim is here."

I stared into her face. "The head monk. I think he is the last victim . . ."

"*Why?* What could possibly give you that idea? How can you possibly know that?"

I grabbed both her shoulders in my hands. "Because the killer is trying to bring these people to enlightenment! I don't know why! But this killer is trying to create Buddhas!"

The door opened, and Bhante Bhavana Dhana stood frowning at me. He turned deliberately to Dehan and then back to me again.

"Detective, we can hear you. There is no need to break down the door. What do you want?"

"I need to see Bhante Bodhisattva Adhiṭṭhāna, and I need to see him now."

"I am very sorry that you have this need, Detective, because it is not possible for you to see him."

I growled, "Why not?"

"Because he is not with us. He has gone."

"You mean he is dead?"

"Not as far as I know, but he has gone to a country retreat for meditation. He will not come back until . . ."

"You don't understand. I need to see him now. His life might be in danger. I think there is somebody planning to kill him. I need to know where he is."

His face didn't change. His expression remained impassive. But he stepped back into the shadows of the hall so that his face disappeared from view, save his eyes. He said, "Please, come in out of the rain. I will give you his address and his cell number."

We went inside. The place was still and quiet. The closing door shut out the tapping of the rain. A dim light was on in the hall, and Bhante Bhavana Dhana leaned into the small library and flipped on the light. He stepped back and gestured us to enter.

"Please, sit. I will get what you want."

He disappeared down a passage, and we moved into the library. Dehan sat on the small sofa where I had sat earlier. Her face was drawn, and her eyes were worried as she looked up at me.

"Are you sure about this, Stone? Are you sure we're not just clutching at straws?"

I stared at her face a moment, wondering if she was right, then shook my head. "Think it through. Our first premise has to be that these killings are motivated by some kind of mystical belief. It is the only way we can explain the changing MO, and the music.

Each one is chosen to fit the victim. Once we accept that, we have a choice: either they are punishment killings, or, for want of a better name, mercy killings. If they are punishment killings, we keep coming up against the problem of Georgina Cheng. She is different in every way to the others. It only makes sense to kill her if the victims have been chosen for what they can become, rather than what they have been."

She gave her head a small shake. "I don't know, Stone. Yeah, your words make sense, but we seem to be way out there."

"I know, Dehan, but keep thinking. Things that all the victims had in common, a search, a . . ." I looked around the library, trying to find the right word. "A drive, however misguided, to find a solution to suffering. For Cavendish it was atheism and eventually Buddhism, an attempt to see reality as it is. For Judge Jones it was justice; for Georgina it was medicine, and vivisection was a necessary sacrifice—all of them were looking for the same thing Buddhism says the Buddha was looking for: a way out of pain and suffering. That is the one thing that unites them all, and along the way they crossed the paths of Reverend Wells and Sam Ogden, Bhante Bodhisattva Adhiṭṭhāna."

She puffed out her cheeks and blew noisily. "So who the hell is doing this, Stone? Who is our suspect?"

I shook my head. "I don't know. Someone with a twisted understanding of Buddhism."

A soft noise behind me made me turn. Bhante Bhavana Dhana was in the doorway, looking at me with his large, expressionless eyes. He reached out his hand, and there was a card in it.

"It is a small retreat on Long Island. A gift. We can go there to retreat and meditate, and also run courses. Bhante Bodhisattva Adhiṭṭhāna is there now." He put his hands together and gave a small bow. "In Buddhism, we do not talk about meditation. This is Christian concept, like contemplation. In Buddhism we talk about training the mind to concentrate, to see things as they really are. Bhante Bodhisattva Adhiṭṭhāna has very powerful, clear mind." He searched my eyes for a moment. I was frowning, struggling to grasp what he was telling me. He went on. "In Buddhism, also, we do not talk about reincarnation"—he laughed—"entering once again the meat! In Buddhism we talk about 're-becoming,' for we become new again at every moment, at every 'now.' We must all die, Detective, but death is not the end. Death is re-becoming, and when Bhante Bodhisattva Adhiṭṭhāna becomes new, maybe he will be ready for buddhata, that is Buddhahood, or Buddha nature. Go in peace, help him if you can."

My skin had turned cold, and I felt my hairs stand on end. I didn't answer him. I went fast for the door, wrenched it open, and ran out into the rain. I could hear Dehan running behind me. I clambered into the Jag while she ran around the hood and slipped in the other side. The headlamps came on, driving shafts of light through the glistening drops of falling rain. I spun the wheel and turned, sweeping the beams through a wide arc, and accelerated back toward Soundview while Dehan put the magnetic light on the dash and connected the siren.

I took White Plains at the fork before O'Brien and skidded onto Bruckner Boulevard doing fifty, but the Jaguar held the road, and we rocketed on to exit 54 toward Throggs Neck. It was almost five miles to the next serious bend, and, despite the rain, I crossed the toll bridge doing 125. I knew that in normal conditions it was a two-and-a-half-hour drive, and even if I cut it by half an hour, it still gave the killer a two-hour lead. I felt sick with anxiety but fought to stay cool and focused.

At Alley Park we took the exit to the Long Island Expressway and started the long, near-straight drive to Montauk, at the eastern tip of the island. It was over a hundred miles, and I had to do it in less than an hour. The Mark II had a four-speed manual gearshift and a top speed of 125 miles per hour. And despite being fifty-six years old, because of its low stance and the genius of its designers, it held the road like it had claws.

As it was, I only shaved five minutes off the hour, and we slowed toward the Montauk Point Lighthouse Museum at ten minutes before nine. We rounded the bend, passed the restaurant, and took the right fork that led down through woodland and shrubs toward the beach.

After half a mile of rolling and bumping over uneven, pitted blacktop, the amber light of the headlamps picked out a large, double-fronted house set back from the road among sand dunes and heather, with the back of the building lost among the black silhouettes of trees. There was a gate that stood open. Beside it was a wooden sign that read simply, *Buddhist Retreat*. A dirt track served as a drive up to the front of the house.

There were no lights visible at first, but the glow of the headlamps picked out wooden steps that rose to a wooden porch. I killed the engine, and we climbed out. The slamming doors caused a jarring echo in the silence. The surf sighed in the distance and cooled the breeze. Dehan climbed the steps and rang the bell while I walked around the side and back of the house, staring up at the windows for signs of life.

At first it seemed all the windows were dark, and I wondered if Bhante Bhavana Dhana had sent us deliberately on a wild goose chase. But then, in back of the house, I saw a window at the far end. It was a sash that stood halfway open, and inside I could see the flickering light of candles. I listened hard. All I could hear was the whisper of the surf, the sigh of the sea breeze in the trees, and far off an owl calling for a mate. I turned and walked quickly back to Dehan. She was ringing the bell again.

I said, "In back, there's a window open, and I can see candlelight."

"Any music?"

I shook my head and hammered hard on the door. There was no answer.

"Will he come if he's meditating?"

I shrugged. "I have no idea. You'd better go round back and shout to him. I'll keep hammering."

But a minute of pounding the door brought nothing, and when Dehan came back and said she'd had no answer either, I began to feel anxiety twisting up in my gut again. I pulled my piece from my holster. Dehan held out a hand and said, "Wait."

She turned the handle, and the door swung open. I gave her a rueful smile, and she held up a finger. "*Entia non sunt multiplicanda praeter necesitatem,* Occam's razor. Don't complicate your life."

I stepped inside and flipped the switch. Nothing happened. I stood a moment, allowing my eyes to adjust to the darkness. Gradually a broad, sparsely furnished living room with wooden floors and walls, populated by dark, amorphous shadows, came into partial focus. I took out my flashlight and played the beam over the mahogany staircase. I crossed the room and climbed the stairs to the upper floor. There I found a wide landing with a window overlooking the East River. A fat, orange moon was warping out of the horizon, tainting the black water with liquid gobbets of light.

There were doors to my left, which I ignored. Across the landing to my right, there was one door that held my attention. It was closed, but along the crack at the bottom I could see the flickering orange light of candles. I didn't hesitate. I crossed the landing, turned the handle, and opened the door.

Bhante Bodhisattva Adhiṭṭhāna was sitting in the lotus position on a woven blanket on the floor. His eyes were closed, and his expression was one of absolute peace. He was surrounded by nine candles, and through the open window the sound of the ocean, the breeze, and the owl were clear.

I said, "Bhante, your life is at risk. You need to come with us."

His eyes opened and fastened on mine like two vices. His concentration was like a physical thing. I could feel the power of his mind.

"Life, Detective, does not belong to anyone. Life is."

"You don't understand. There is somebody trying to kill you!"

"I understand, Detective, but you do not. There is no 'I' to be killed, there is no death to deal, there is no single life to be lost. Be at peace, Detective. You have found what you seek, and you do not even know it."

The room swayed, my mind rocked, and my eyes registered for the first time the two-gallon cans of gasoline perched on the edge of a table above three of the candles. They were suspended from ropes that were slowly burning, singed by the flames. I heard my voice, loud and distorted, "*No!*"

Dehan grabbed me, and I knew I had lunged for him. I heard her voice loud in my ear, "*Stone! No! You'll spill the canisters!*"

He had raised his right hand, palm out.

"Do not come in, Detective Stone. The rope is thin; any disturbance could break it and you could be injured. That is not my intent. If you have questions, make them fast; time is coming to an end."

My head was reeling. "You killed them! You killed all of them!"

"I killed each one."

"No forced entries. They let you in because they trusted you. But, *why*? You spoke about compassion, about loving kindness, about avoiding pain and suffering . . ."

"And how do we do that, Detective? Only by achieving Buddha Nature can we escape the eternal cycle of suffering, of craving and aversion, of pain. So I have brought freedom from suffering to eight people. I shall be the ninth."

A sudden rage welled up inside me, and I roared, "*But you tortured these people! Jensen was a kind, harmless man! The reverend was good and humane! What right had you to torture them and rob them of their lives?*"

His smile was peaceful and immutable. "I chose a death and a meditation for each one, so that they would detach from suffering while dying, and so achieve buddhata, enlightenment, in their next life."

"The music . . ."

"The music, and a mantra I gave each one. Each was designed so that their dying thoughts would be of liberation from suffering and achieving awakening. Do you see, Detective, what I have done?"

I shook my head. I felt an indescribable grief and betrayal. "I see that you have betrayed a sacred trust, I see that you have tortured and murdered eight innocent people . . ."

His eyes were closed, and he was shaking his head. "Time is about to stop, Detective." His eyes snapped open, and he held me in their grip. "I have created nine Buddhas! When we return, we will bring with us an age of peace." He closed his eyes again. A slow groan escaped his throat and he said, "Now, run!"

There was a snap, followed by a strangely banal, plastic clatter. We both stood, paralyzed as we listened to the gurgle and watched the pungent liquid spill and spread. I noticed then, for the first time, the small candle he had in front of him, the small piece of cloth that trailed from it, the long tongue of lethal liquid running across the floor toward it.

I heard in my mind, as loud as though it had been real, Bhante Bodhisattva Adhiṭṭhāna's voice bellow at me, "*Now, run!*"

I grabbed Dehan's arm and dragged her from the room, propelling her across the landing to the top of the stairs. There was an almighty *whoosh!* behind us as the gasoline caught and the room was filled with light. I screamed at Dehan, "*Get out! Go down! Call 911!*" and I ran back toward the door. The heat gushing from the room was overpowering and hurled me back. As I raised my arms to protect my face, I saw my cuffs singed and smoldering. I cowered away. Somewhere I heard a voice screaming, "*Bhante! Bhante!*" and realized it was my own. Gas fumes concentrated in the two cans must have ignited then, because there were two massive reports, and a blast of scorching air threw me to the floor. As I struggled to rise, with my jacket singed and smoking, I saw the immobile figure of Bhante Bodhisattva Adhiṭṭhāna, Sam Ogden, sitting in the lotus position, engulfed in flames.

Then two powerful hands grabbed me by the collar and dragged me to the stairs. I stumbled to my feet. A voice—not my own, but Dehan's—was screaming at me, "*Run! Run!*" and she dragged me stumbling down the stairs toward the front door. Above us, long tongues of flame licked out of the room, catching the ancient dry wood of the old building and devouring it like a hungry daemon. We fell out of the door, down the old steps, and collapsed in the sodden sand and grass.

The flames spread at a frightening speed, punching out the glass from the windows and licking up the sides of the house. Soon the building was a roaring mass of flames whose light danced on the dark water of the beach, reaching out toward the rising moon.

I looked at Dehan, with the orange flames washing unsteadily across her face, flickering in her eyes. "Why the hell did you go back?" she asked me.

I couldn't answer her. All I could say was, "Is he dead? He must be dead by now . . ."

I looked back at the huge hulk of flames, the roaring furnace that he had created, and reeled away from the thought of his body still living in that hell. We got to our feet and backed away toward the gate, where we had left the Jaguar. Dehan was calling 911, but already we could hear sirens beginning to wail into the dark night.

EPILOGUE

LATER, MUCH LATER, AS DAWN WAS RISING GRAY OVER the East River, and the last of the fire trucks was pulling away, I sat beside Dehan on a sand dune, looking at the smoldering wreck that had been Bhante Bodhisattva Adhiṭṭhāna's Buddhist retreat, a place to find truth and peace, escape pain and suffering, and see things as they really were.

Dehan's head was on my shoulder, and she was hugging my right arm with both of hers.

"Is it true, do you think?" I asked. "Are we born again? Do we re-become, according to our last thoughts?"

"I don't know, Stone. I was brought up by a Catholic and a Jew, but I think I'm probably an agnostic atheist. For us it's either total fatalism or Daddy will take care of everything. I've never really thought about death. I was always too busy with life."

"But death comes." I explored her beautiful face for a moment. "Our careers, Dehan, are built on investigating death, but . . ." I shook my head. "We have no idea what it is. And yet it comes. It's relentless."

She put her chin on my shoulder to look up at me. "It's a few years off, big guy."

I nodded. "It was for eight people whose souls were snatched to become Buddhas. It was for Sam Ogden . . ." I shook my head. "How could I have got it so wrong?"

"But he chose what happened to him, Stone."

"Maybe," I said, "maybe that was the point."

"What do you mean?"

I stared for a while at the smoldering wreckage of the Buddhist retreat. A long snake of smoke coiled up into the dawn light.

"All of those people had pinned their hopes, their lives, their futures on something external, from Schrödinger's cat to justice and the law to God, even to Buddhism and Sam Ogden. They were all living by accident, reacting to what happened outside in the world around them. Sam Ogden, however crazy he might have been, however immoral what he did may have been, was the only one who was living on purpose. He knew exactly what he was doing, and he took the consequences and responsibility onto himself, without laying blame, or his life, at anybody else's doorstep."

She raised her head and stared at me. "Hell, Stone! I hope you're not justifying what he did!"

I shook my head. "No. Not at all. But that's just the point. He doesn't need me to justify it. Because he did it on purpose. He was living and thinking on purpose."

"You think that matters?"

It took me a while to answer. When I did, it wasn't much of an answer. I said, "I don't know. Because I can't see things as they really are. But I have a hunch that maybe, maybe thinking—and living—on purpose is important."

We stood and half walked, half slid down the dune to the path where the old burgundy bruiser was waiting. Dehan climbed in, and I took a moment to lean on the roof and look one last time at the smoldering remains of the refuge where Bhante Bodhisattva Adhiṭṭhāna's ashes lay. A breeze moved in from the East River and stirred the embers of the temple, and suddenly a flame licked up out of the timbers, erupted into a ball of fire, and exploded up toward the sky.

I climbed in behind the wheel and smiled at Dehan's beautiful face. I drew breath to make a meaningless remark about going home, but she spoke first and quoted the Bard, words that had no time or place, but timeless meaning.

"There is no right or wrong," she said, "but thinking makes it so." And in the silence of the cab she added, from *Paradise Lost*, "And the mind is its own place."

Don't miss KNIFE EDGE. The riveting sequel in the Dead Cold Mystery series.

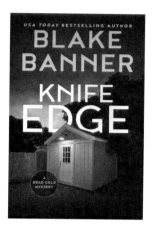

Scan the QR code below to purchase KNIFE EDGE

Or go to: righthouse.com/knife-edge

NOTE: flip to the very end to read an exclusive sneak peak...

DON'T MISS ANYTHING!

If you want to stay up to date on all new releases in this series, with this author, or with any of our new deals, you can do so by joining our newsletters below.

In addition, you will immediately gain access to our entire *Right House VIP Library,* which includes many riveting Mystery and Thriller novels for your enjoyment!

righthouse.com/email

(Easy to unsubscribe. No spam. Ever.)

ALSO BY BLAKE BANNER

Up to date books can be found at:
www.righthouse.com/blake-banner

ROGUE THRILLERS
Gates of Hell (Book 1)
Hell's Fury (Book 2)

ALEX MASON THRILLERS
Odin (Book 1)
Ice Cold Spy (Book 2)
Mason's Law (Book 3)
Assets and Liabilities (Book 4)
Russian Roulette (Book 5)
Executive Order (Book 6)
Dead Man Talking (Book 7)
All The King's Men (Book 8)
Flashpoint (Book 9)
Brotherhood of the Goat (Book 10)
Dead Hot (Book 11)
Blood on Megiddo (Book 12)
Son of Hell (Book 13)

HARRY BAUER THRILLER SERIES
Dead of Night (Book 1)
Dying Breath (Book 2)
The Einstaat Brief (Book 3)
Quantum Kill (Book 4)
Immortal Hate (Book 5)
The Silent Blade (Book 6)
LA: Wild Justice (Book 7)

Breath of Hell (Book 8)
Invisible Evil (Book 9)
The Shadow of Ukupacha (Book 10)
Sweet Razor Cut (Book 11)
Blood of the Innocent (Book 12)
Blood on Balthazar (Book 13)
Simple Kill (Book 14)
Riding The Devil (Book 15)
The Unavenged (Book 16)
The Devil's Vengeance (Book 17)
Bloody Retribution (Book 18)
Rogue Kill (Book 19)
Blood for Blood (Book 20)

DEAD COLD MYSTERY SERIES

An Ace and a Pair (Book 1)
Two Bare Arms (Book 2)
Garden of the Damned (Book 3)
Let Us Prey (Book 4)
The Sins of the Father (Book 5)
Strange and Sinister Path (Book 6)
The Heart to Kill (Book 7)
Unnatural Murder (Book 8)
Fire from Heaven (Book 9)
To Kill Upon A Kiss (Book 10)
Murder Most Scottish (Book 11)
The Butcher of Whitechapel (Book 12)
Little Dead Riding Hood (Book 13)
Trick or Treat (Book 14)
Blood Into Wine (Book 15)
Jack In The Box (Book 16)
The Fall Moon (Book 17)
Blood In Babylon (Book 18)
Death In Dexter (Book 19)
Mustang Sally (Book 20)

ABOUT US

Right House is an independent publisher created by authors for readers. We specialize in Action, Thriller, Mystery, and Crime novels.

If you enjoyed this novel, then there is a good chance you will like what else we have to offer! Please stay up to date by using any of the links below.

Join our mailing lists to stay up to date -->
righthouse.com/email
Visit our website --> righthouse.com
Contact us --> contact@righthouse.com

facebook.com/righthousebooks
x.com/righthousebooks
instagram.com/righthousebooks

EXCLUSIVE SNEAK PEAK OF...

KNIFE EDGE

CHAPTER 1

"I WISH," SHE SAID, "IT WAS AS EASY AS JUST BEING color-blind. But the problem isn't really that the color of our skin is different. It isn't even a question of race. It's much deeper than that. And however hard the Mitchells tried, at the end of the day, they were the mighty white intellectuals, and Leroy was a black orphan they were trying to rescue. They tried not to see it that way, but that was the way Leroy saw it."

She paused and gazed down at her Styrofoam cup on the Formica interrogation-room table. It was a sad gaze in a beautiful face. She turned the cup around several times, like she was trying to find some redeeming feature about it but knew she wouldn't. In the end it was just a white Styrofoam cup full of black coffee.

"I guess that sounds selfish and ungrateful to you, but to a lot of black people, charity and help is like the final insult." She raised large, black eyes to look at me. "White people brought us to this condition, now they want to tell us, 'You will never make it alone, you need white men to achieve anything.'" She paused again and returned her gaze to the cup. "I didn't see it that way. I don't. I was grateful, especially to Emma Mitchell. She took Leroy into her family, into her home, like he was her own child. At least, she tried real hard to make it seem that way. Though he never really believed it. Trust was hard for him."

"What made it hard for him to trust, Sonia?"

She thought about it. "I should start from the beginning."

"I'd be grateful. I am not familiar with this case."

She sighed and sagged back in her chair. She thought for a moment and said, "My sister, Cherise, she got involved with this man. I say 'man' for want of a better word. Earl Brown, he was no good"—she darted me a glance—"like so many men, I am afraid to say. He always had a bottle in his hand, beer, whiskey, whatever. And in the other hand he always had a joint. What he never had was a steady job, and if ever he got one, he made damn sure it didn't last. He was a bad man, but we didn't realize how bad he was until it was too late."

"What happened?"

"She had two children by him, Leroy and Shevron. Like I said, he was never at work. He was at home all the time, watching TV, drinking, and smoking weed. So it was *she* had to go out to work to feed the family and keep a roof over their heads." She paused to stare at the wall. "Eight years they went on like that. I told her, more times than I can remember, 'You have got to get rid of that man, Cherise! You have got to be *free* of that man!' But she never listened. Women can be just as stupid as men sometimes. She made excuses for him, justified him, and supported that evil parasite right to the end."

She paused again and took a deep breath. "One day, I remember it like it was just yesterday: May 14, 2010, she come home early from work because she didn't feel well. She was sick. She opened the door, the front door of the house, it opened right onto the living room from the street, and she sees Leroy sitting in the armchair watching his daddy rape his little sister, Shevron. She's only six years old, and that bastard was there raping her. Well, it turned out later, he'd been doing that for years, to both of the kids."

"So what did your sister do?"

"What did she do? What would you do? What would I do? What would anybody do? She dropped her bag and ran for the kitchen. She grabbed the kitchen knife and ran at him, screaming like a wild thing. They had an almighty fight."

She shook her head. Her bottom lip curled in, and tears balanced on her eyelids then spilled onto her cheek.

"It's ten years ago, maybe more, but it feels like it was just this morning. There was a big fight. A real big fight. Little Shevron tried to protect her mother, and that bastard killed her for it, hit her so hard he broke her neck. Then, it seems, Cherise stabbed Earl in the back with the kitchen knife. Should have killed him, but somehow he took it from her and stabbed her several times in the belly, in some kind of frenzy, before he collapsed and they both died."

I frowned and raised a hand to stop her. "How do you know this, Sonia?"

She nodded, as though she agreed with the question. "Leroy was so traumatized his memory was pretty vague, but he witnessed everything. Also, the medical examiner and the investigating detectives pieced it all together that way, by the position of the bodies and where the wounds were. And it all made sense. It was the only way it could have happened."

She paused, gathering her thoughts.

"Several of the neighbors called the cops when they heard the screams and shouts. I think there was a couple of them the cops were interested in for a while, but they had alibis, and in the end they figured it went down the way they said, they killed each other and left poor Leroy alone in the world."

"You didn't adopt him?"

"I couldn't. I live alone and I work long hours. There was no way I could afford the money or the time to look after a traumatized kid of eight." She shook her head, confirming the impossibility. "No, he went to the orphanage. But not for long. The Mitchells had read about the murder, they live in the Bronx, and they offered to adopt him. They changed his name. Dr. Mitchell,

Brad, said it would help him to reinvent himself after the trauma, but I believe it just sounded less black to them than Leroy."

"What can you tell me about the Mitchells?"

"They are both academics. They lecture at NYU, he is a psychiatrist, I think, and she is in sociology or women's studies or something like that. Anyhow, there was a lot of debate and discussion about whether a white family should adopt a black kid. Brad accused the orphanage of instigating apartheid through the back door and said he would sue them and have them shut down, so they agreed to approve the adoption, and Leroy went to live with them about six months after the murder."

I cleared my throat and scratched my head. "Was he seeing a therapist of any sort at that time?"

"Yes, the court appointed a child psychologist to see him on a regular basis. Ms. Simone Robles. He saw her once a week to begin with, but it was less than that, about once a month, by the time . . ."

She hesitated. She looked away, blinking.

"Let's stay with his move to the Mitchells for now. He was what, eight, nine?"

"He was still only eight."

"How did he get on with the Mitchells? They had children of their own?"

She nodded. "They were very nice to him, and at first he appreciated that. They were good, kind people, especially Emma. With Brad, even though he was a good man, you always felt he was doing what he was doing out of a sense of principle, or obligation. He believed he should be doing it, so he did it. But with Emma . . ." She smiled. "With her you felt it was more from the heart. She was warmer."

"They had kids?" I asked again.

"They had two kids, a little younger than Leroy. There was Marcus, who was about six or seven, and Lea, who was four or five."

"And how did Leroy get on with Marcus and Lea?"

She nodded several times, looking down at the Formica top of the table. Eventually she said, "They got on well. He was maybe too keen to please, too excitable, but the whole family was kind and patient and tolerant, and very slowly he began to settle down into the family. Marcus was real kind to him, called him his brother. Everything was fine, or at least it seemed to be fine."

"You mean it wasn't? Was there something you didn't know about?"

She heaved a big, heavy sigh. "I don't know. For four years he seemed to be happy, in as much as he could be. But when he turned twelve, in August 2013, his attitude started to change. He started talking a lot of stupid crap about blacks and whites, about how black men were better and stronger than white men, about how white women preferred black men—I don't know where he was getting that stuff, but it began to worry me."

"He was in touch with you, obviously."

"He used to come visit with me. Sometimes he'd stay the weekend. We used to write WhatsApp messages to each other. He loved his aunt"—she smiled—"but when I told him he was talking a lot of BS, and that God made all men and women equal, he told me I didn't know what I was talking about. That made me unhappy. I told him I did not want him talking like that in front of the Mitchells. He promised me he wouldn't, but I didn't really believe him.

"I spoke to Emma about it once, and she told me not to worry about it. She said he had had a very traumatic experience and it would take him years to deal with it and come to terms with it. What he was doing with all that racist rubbish was to try and find his own identity, his own sense of self, and for that he would have to go through a lot of garbage. She was a wonderful woman, Detective Stone."

"So what happened?"

"Just about a week after we talked, I got a phone call from Emma. She told me Leroy had been killed, and so had her little girl, Lea. Marcus had not been hurt"—she jabbed at her body with her fingertips—"physically, but he was in a bad state of shock, and he was being seen by a psychiatrist."

The story was new to me. I had vague memories of having read something about it, and hearing talk at the station house, but I had not retained any of the details. I frowned. "How were they killed?"

"It was Sunday, June 13. Brad and Emma had been sitting drinking coffee after breakfast and the kids were playing in the backyard. It was a big area." She stretched out her hands to indicate it was large. "They had a big lawn with trees at the end, and flower beds and stuff, and they had a garden shed where they kept the gardening tools and flowerpots . . ." She trailed off.

"What happened?"

"They were having coffee, like I said, and suddenly they heard a lot of screaming. Brad said it sounded hysterical. They recognized the voices of the kids, and they ran to see what was going on. According to Brad, the voices were coming from the garden shed. They rushed to see what had happened, thinking maybe one of the kids had hurt themselves with one of the tools. But it was much worse than that."

She placed her fingertips over her mouth, as though she was receiving the shock all over again. She closed her eyes and spoke in a strange monotone, like some kind of android.

"They found Lea and Leroy dead on the floor of the shed. Emma said there was blood everywhere. The floor was thick . . ." She shook her head without opening her eyes. "Thick, with blood. Lea had had her throat cut, and Leroy had been stabbed in the back, repeatedly, as if in a frenzy."

"What about . . ." I checked my notes. "Marcus? Where was Marcus?"

"They found him, poor kid, they found him hiding under a tarp in the shed. He was shivering, and the ME said he was in a deep state of shock. He couldn't speak."

"But"—my frown deepened—"they must have spoken to him eventually. What did he say had happened?"

She shook her head. "No, the doctor said he needed time to get over the shock, but he gradually slipped into a catatonic depression, which just got worse. He never spoke again—from that morning on, till now, he hasn't said a word. And as far as I know he hasn't got out of bed."

I scribbled some notes and asked, "What was the outcome of the investigation, do you know?"

"It was never solved. There was no DNA other than the kids', nor any . . ." She made little flapping motions with her hand.

I said, "Forensic evidence?"

She nodded. "Yes, forensic evidence. And the only witness, as far as they could tell, was Marcus. And he wasn't talking. So the case went cold."

I leaned back in my chair and tapped my pen on my notepad.

"As far as I can tell, from what you've told me, Sonia, there is nothing new here. You've described the two murders, very clearly and concisely"—I smiled at her—"and thank you for that, but there is nothing new. Unless we have some fresh evidence, it is hard to see how we can go any further with the investigation."

She nodded at her hands clasped on the table, but she didn't move. I watched her narrowly for a moment, then went on.

"But you didn't come here after six years just to repeat to me what I could have found in the file. Has something new come up? Is there something that wasn't mentioned in the original investigation?"

She sighed again. "Not exactly. You see . . ." She stopped, then started again. "I told you that Leroy started going through a difficult phase, where he was rebelling against Brad and Emma."

"Sure, it didn't seem to worry them too much."

"Well, what they didn't know was that he wrote me a text message one day, a couple of weeks before . . ." She faltered again.

I said, "Before the crime."

"Yes, before the crime. In that message he said that he knew Brad was seeing another woman. He'd heard him on the phone, talking quietly, and he said he'd seen messages. So he cut school a couple of times and went to the university, where he said he saw Brad with another woman." She reached in her purse and pulled out a cell. She opened her photographs and slid the phone across the table to me. "He sent me this picture."

It showed a tall, slim man in his early forties. He was wearing a tweed jacket and chinos and had a shock of prematurely white hair swept back from his face. He was smiling, talking to an attractive woman in her early thirties. By their expressions you'd guess they liked each other, but not much more than that. I gave my head a shake and looked at her.

"I'm afraid this proves nothing, Sonia. A university professor must speak to hundreds of people every week."

"I know, and that's why I never mentioned it at the time. I put it down to Leroy's feelings of rebellion and inadequacy about Brad. He said he was going to use the photograph to blackmail Brad. I got real mad and scolded him, and told him he should be ashamed of himself, and to be honest I never thought any more about it until last week."

"What happened last week?"

"A friend of mine at work pointed it out to me. It was an article in the paper. Brad Mitchell has opened a rehab clinic upstate, beyond White Plains, in the Silver Lake Preserve." She stopped again, rubbing the fingers of her right hand with her left.

I asked, "And . . . ?"

"The psychiatrist in charge of the Mitchell Clinic will be Dr. Margaret Wagner, the woman in that photograph."

I winced. It was close, but not close enough. "In itself," I said, "if they are colleagues, there is nothing odd about that. If they have been working together for five or six years, perhaps much longer, you would expect him to name her, a close, trusted colleague, over somebody else."

She was nodding. "Yeah, I know, and that's why I didn't come straight here. But I kept asking myself, what if there was something in what Leroy saw and heard? What if when Leroy saw them together, they were a lot more intimate than what comes across in that picture? What if he went to Brad Mitchell and did try to blackmail him? That was only six years ago; maybe they were already planning their clinic for celebrity drug addicts. That little black brat, he could have screwed it up for them for good."

I puffed out my cheeks and blew. She shook her head again. "I am not saying that's what happened. I am just asking, what if?"

I thought about it for a long moment.

"Okay, Sonia, send me the picture, I'll discuss it with my partner, and maybe we'll review the case and go and have a talk with Brad Mitchell and Dr. Wagner. I can't promise you anything, but we'll have a look and see if the lead is worth following."

She smiled and thanked me, and sat a moment. I figured she was in her late forties. She was attractive and elegant but looked tired, drawn, and unhappy. Finally she stood and left, and I reached for my cell.

CHAPTER 2

THE PHONE RANG THREE TIMES BEFORE SHE PICKED IT up. When she spoke, she was out of breath.

"Yeah, Stone, what's up?"

"Where are you?"

"I'm working out in the gym, why?"

"Because we're going to visit Brad and Emma Mitchell, in Castle Hill."

"Uh-huh. Why?"

"Git yer ass up to your desk and you can read why in the file."

I heard a soft grunt. "I love when you talk rough like that, you bad, bad man."

I hung up and went down to my desk to sort through our cardboard filing system, comprised of two large cartons, and found *Brown 2010*, and *Mitchell 2014*. They were cross-referenced. I read them over briefly, called Frank, the ME, about something I didn't understand, and was making copies of the two files when Dehan walked in, looking fresh and lithe. I shoved a file in her hands.

"One," I said.

"Hello."

I ignored her and went on. "Cherise Brown, married to Earl

Brown, like so many men, a no-good, low-down drunk. She, apparently blinded by love, had two children by him, Leroy and Shevron. While he was at home watching TV, drinking whiskey, and smoking weed, she was at work raising money to feed her family. This went on for eight years. Her sister, Sonia, our informant, advised her repeatedly to leave him and start a new life, but Cherise made excuses for him, and they stayed together."

Dehan rested her ass on the side of her desk and frowned at me. I went on.

"On May 14, 2010, Cherise arrived home early from work and found Earl raping six-year-old Shevron while eight-year-old Leroy watched. It turned out later this had been going on for some years, to both of the kids."

"Son of a bitch. What did Mom do?"

"She went to the kitchen, grabbed the kitchen knife, and attacked him. There was a fight."

"In front of the kids?"

"Mm-hm, Shevron tried to protect her mother and Earl hit her so hard he broke her neck. Reconstruction by the ME and the detectives at the time was that Cherise stabbed Earl in the back, he somehow took the knife from her and stabbed her several times in the belly before collapsing, and they both died."

"Leaving Leroy as the only living witness to the violent death of his entire family. Holy sh . . ."

I nodded. "But that's not all of it."

"There's more?"

"Yup." I collected up the copies and dropped into my chair at the desk. She shifted round to look at me. "Leroy went to an orphanage for about six months. Almost immediately, as soon as the murder was reported in the press, the Mitchells, a liberal, academic family who were residents of the Bronx, applied to adopt Leroy. They both lectured at NYU. He's a psychiatrist, she a sociologist. There was some concern about whether a white family should adopt a black orphan, but after six months and threats of legal action, it was approved."

"Kid had a shrink?"

"Simone Robles. In the file. He was still only eight."

"The Mitchells had kids?"

"Two kids, younger than Leroy. Marcus, seven, and Lea, five. Apparently they got on well, and the whole family was keen to make it work. Seems the kids liked each other, but . . ."

"There had to be a but."

"It seems, when Leroy turned twelve, in August 2013, he began to change. He started talking to his aunt about how black men were better and stronger than white men, how white women preferred black men. He used to write her WhatsApp messages on the subject. Sonia spoke to Emma about it, but the Mitchells didn't seem too concerned. They thought it was normal given the trauma he had suffered, and he'd get over it . . ."

"So what happened?"

"On June 13, four years and a month, almost to the day, after his parents and his sister were killed, he was killed too, along with his adoptive sister, Lea."

"Holy cow. How were they killed?"

"It was a Sunday, Brad and Emma Mitchell had been drinking coffee after breakfast and the kids were playing in the backyard. They had a big lawn and a garden shed where they kept the gardening tools. At some point, the Mitchells started to hear a lot of screaming coming from the shed. They ran to see what it was about and found Lea and Leroy dead. There was a lot of blood on the floor. Lea had had her throat cut, and Leroy had been stabbed repeatedly in the back."

Dehan was frowning hard. "What about the other boy, Marcus?"

"They found him in the shed, hiding under a tarpaulin. He was in severe shock. He hasn't been able to help as a witness because he slipped into a catatonic depression and never really recovered. He has never spoken again, to this day."

"Huh!"

"It was never solved. There was no DNA or forensic evidence, and the case went cold."

She nodded. "And the only witness was the kid, Marcus."

"Yup."

"Okay . . ." She moved around to her chair and sat in it. "But I don't see how we can do anything with this, Stone. Where the hell do you begin?"

I leaned forward with my elbows on the desk. "Sonia came to see me this morning, and she brought not so much new evidence as old evidence with a new angle. It's thin, but . . ." I shrugged. "I think it's worth a look. It seems, a couple of weeks before he was killed, Leroy—or Lee, as his new family called him—sent a WhatsApp message to his aunt telling her that he thought Brad Mitchell was having an affair. He'd heard him on the phone and, apparently, he'd seen text messages. So he'd cut school a couple of times and been to the university, where he'd seen Brad with that woman." I slid my cell across the table to her. "He sent her this picture."

She glanced at it. "So what? Proves nothing. It's not even suggestive."

"Yeah, agreed. But Sonia and a workmate found an article in the paper which said that Brad Mitchell had opened a rehab clinic near White Plains, in the Silver Lake Preserve. The psychiatrist in charge of the Mitchell Clinic was to be Dr. Margaret Wagner, the woman in that photograph."

She sagged back in her chair, made a wincing face, and blew. "You're right. It's thin. It's not thin, it's anorexic supermodel skinny."

"Yeah, I know, but Sonia makes the point, and I agree, Leroy threatened to blackmail Brad Mitchell. If the clinic was already on the cards back then, that's a pretty strong motive for murder. Especially if the victim is not your own kid, but an increasingly obnoxious intruder."

She screwed skepticism into her face. "But he'd also have to have killed his own daughter. And his wife says they were having coffee together. She's not likely to alibi him if he's killed her daughter."

I shrugged. "Yeah, but like Sonia said, what if? I think it's worth asking a few questions and finding out exactly what kind of relationship he and Dr. Wagner have."

She turned a pencil around in her fingers for a while, then said, "Yeah, I guess. So where do we start, with Dr. Wagner?"

"Yes, chances are she knows nothing about the kid's death. But all we want from her is whether she was having an affair with Mitchell. If we catch her off guard she might just come clean. If we go to Mitchell first, he'll alert her, and she could clam up."

She nodded and made to stand. "So all we are doing right now is establishing whether she and Brad Mitchell were having an affair."

"Correct."

"And then we take it from there?"

"Yup."

"Okay."

She flicked through her phone book and after a moment made a call. She sat staring at me for a moment with the phone to her ear, biting her lip. Then:

"Yeah, good morning, this is Detective Carmen Dehan of the NYPD. We would like to meet with the director of the clinic . . . Dr. Margaret Wagner? Okay, thanks." She winked at me and mouthed *putting me through to her secretary*. "Yeah, good afternoon. Detective Carmen Dehan of the New York Police Department. We would like to meet with the director of the clinic . . . Dr. Margaret Wagner? Let me just make a note . . . Sooner the better. Sure, today, say in about three-quarters of an hour . . . ? Okay, that's great." Another pause, and Dehan pursed her lips and shook her head. "Oh, it's just a routine inquiry. Thanks."

She hung up and smiled. "See, Stone, I'm smart. Now her secretary thinks we had no idea the director was Dr. Wagner, and that our inquiry is about one of her patients. No red flags, no calls to Brad Mitchell."

"You are subtle, Dehan. A subtle, devious, dangerous woman. Let's go."

We stepped out into the cold midmorning light. The sun was low in the south and casting long shadows across Fteley and Story Avenues. We climbed into my ancient burgundy Jaguar Mark II and took the Bronx River Parkway north through endless green suburbs as far as Elmsford, and then turned east into White Plains. It was a half-hour drive, and by the time we got there it was eleven a.m., and the sun was approaching its zenith in a perfect blue sky. We skirted the north of the town and took Hall Avenue into deep woodland. The Brad Mitchell clinic was about a mile in on the right-hand side behind large iron gates set in a fifteen-foot, redbrick wall.

The clinic was an old Georgian manor at the end of a hundred-yard blacktop drive surrounded by sweeping lawns and woodlands. Dehan pushed her shades up onto her head and scrutinized the parkland around us.

"He's not short of a few bucks, Stone. This is a few million in real estate."

I nodded. "Two gets you twenty he has investors, which is further reason to avoid bad publicity."

We pulled up in the parking lot at the front of the building and climbed the flight of six broad granite steps to the main doors. Inside there was the kind of hush you only get with high ceilings and marble floors, where even the echoes seem distant. There was a small, discreet reception desk on the left as we went in. The girl sitting behind it smiled at us with polite indifference and asked Dehan how she could help her.

"We're here to see Dr. Wagner." Dehan showed her her badge, and I showed her mine. "Detectives Carmen Dehan and John Stone."

She picked up a phone on her solid oak desk and after a second said, "Detectives Dehan and Stone to see Dr. Wagner . . . mm-hm." She hung up and pointed to a broad, marble staircase that rose along the back wall of the entrance hall. "Next floor, turn right at the top of the stairs, and Dr. Wagner's office is at the end on the right."

Dehan smiled at her with dead eyes. "If I was a celebrity with a habit, would you take me there yourself?"

The receptionist didn't lose her smile or her composure. She tilted her head on one side and said, "No, Dr. Wagner would come down to meet you."

"That's what I thought."

We turned and climbed the stairs and followed her directions to the end of a long corridor carpeted in red, with prints on the walls depicting English hunt scenes and ships in full sail on the high seas. The door there was open, and through it we found an office paneled in wood, with a desk and a couple of filing cabinets. Behind the desk was a woman in her fifties with gunmetal hair and pale blue eyes that could kill a warm feeling at three hundred paces without blinking. She didn't say hello; she said, "May I see your identification, please?"

We showed her our badges, which she inspected briefly before adding, "Dr. Wagner can spare you ten minutes. Please keep the interview as brief as possible."

Neither of us answered, so she stood, moved to the door that was behind her desk and to the right, knocked, and leaned in.

"The detectives from New York, Dr. Wagner . . ."

She paused a moment, listening, then stood back and held the door open for us. As we filed past, she repeated, under her breath, "Please, keep it brief."

Dehan scowled at her. "Go file something, sister."

Dr. Wagner was standing behind her desk. Your first impression when you looked at her was that you were looking at a very attractive woman. She was tall, and elegant in her movements. She had an abundance of well-cut blond hair, deep, warm brown eyes, and skin that looked naturally youthful. Then you noticed that there were things that were wrong. She was just a bit too tall, her body was boney and angular, and her mouth was too wide. Then you looked again and realized it didn't matter, because in her it all came together and worked. I decided she was a woman a lot of men would find it easy to have an affair with.

I heard the door close behind me and moved across the room. I showed her my badge.

"Dr. Wagner, I am Detective John Stone from the New York Police Department, and this is my partner, Detective Carmen Dehan."

She smiled at Dehan and said, "Congratulations. Female detectives are still a minority. How can I help you? Please, sit down."

This last was also addressed to Dehan. The three of us sat, and I waited for Dehan to speak. Wagner spoke first.

"If it's one of our patients you are interested in, I'm afraid I *will* need a court order. We don't want to be obstructive, and we will give the broadest interpretation to any court order you have, but our patients pay a great deal for our therapies . . ."

Dehan was shaking her head. "We are not here about any of your patients, Dr. Wagner. We are actually here about your relationship with Dr. Brad Mitchell."

She froze. Her eyebrows rose suddenly, and her pale cheeks flushed pink.

"My . . ." She leaned forward slightly. "My *what*?"

Neither of us answered her. We just watched her, trying to read the signs. She laughed and shook her head. "My *relationship* with Dr. Mitchell is purely professional."

Dehan asked, "How long have you known each other?"

"I don't know!" She gazed up and to the left, shaking her head. "Ten, eleven years? Perhaps a little more. Do you mind telling me what this is about?"

Dehan shook her head. "Not at all. How did you meet? Was it at the university?"

She frowned. "Yes. We were in the same department. We were colleagues."

Dehan spread her hands, cocked her head on one side. "A little more than colleagues."

"What do you mean? No, absolutely not! We were colleagues!"

Dehan gestured at the desk with both hands. "He appointed you as the director of his clinic. That is more than just colleagues."

Now she was frowning hard, and her cheeks had deepened to red.

"I don't know what you're driving at, Detective, but there was absolutely no impropriety in my appointment to this position. I worked damn hard for it, and I earned it!"

"I have no doubt about that, Dr. Wagner. I just wanted to make the point that your relationship was not one of mere colleagues. Now that's right, isn't it, Doctor? You were not merely colleagues, were you?"

Dr. Wagner took a deep breath and let it out slow.

"All right, Detective, we were not merely colleagues. We were, and are, also good friends. We tend to play down our friendship because people do love to gossip and spread rumors. But obviously, we planned the clinic from scratch together, and eventually he put up the money, and I run the place. We are not quite partners, but that is on the cards. It is impossible to make that kind of commitment together without becoming close friends . . ."

Dehan was nodding. When Dr. Wagner trailed off, Dehan spoke patiently, almost kindly. "I had got about that far by myself, Doctor. What I am asking you is how close that friendship is."

She hesitated, looked at her desk for a while and then into Dehan's eyes. There was defiance there. "And I am going to ask you again, Detective, what is this about?"

Dehan was about to answer, but I cut in.

"It's about your affair with Dr. Mitchell. We need to know when it started, Dr. Wagner."

Her eyes went wide, and her jaw sagged slightly. Her voice, when she answered, was slightly shrill.

"I don't know where to begin! I mean . . . Quite aside from the fact that I am *not* having an affair with Brad, I *resent* your nosing around in my personal affairs! And *since when* is it the business of the police whether consenting adults have affairs or not?"

I didn't pause or hesitate. "Since those affairs might provide the motive for murder, Dr. Wagner."

"...*Murder?*"

"Yes. This is a murder inquiry, Dr. Wagner. Now, would you please answer the question? When did your affair with Dr. Mitchell begin?"

CHAPTER 3

She sat for a long moment, staring at nothing a couple of inches above her desk. Eventually she frowned at her own thoughts and turned her gaze to me.

"Am I a suspect? I have a right to know. And what about Brad? Is he a suspect?"

Dehan glanced at me. Her face said my play hadn't worked out. I disagreed but shook my head at Dr. Wagner.

"You're not a suspect, Dr. Wagner. Right now we have no real suspects. What we are trying to do is establish the background against which the crime was committed." I offered her a smile which was not unkind and added, "You have already admitted with your silence that you did have an affair with Dr. Mitchell. If you hadn't, you'd have had no problem telling us so, very firmly, I would imagine. What we need to know is when it started and, if it finished, when?"

She was not happy. "If I am not a suspect, I am not under arrest . . ."

I knew where she was going, and so did Dehan. She beat me to the punch and cut her off.

"June 2014, were you together?"

Her face clamped up, but her eyes spoke volumes. Then her mouth joined in. "I think I'd like you to leave now."

I nodded once, looking out of her window at the cold, green landscape, silent and still through triple glazing. "Sure," I said, and shifted my gaze to meet her eyes. "But please bear in mind, Dr. Wagner, that if we decide you are a material witness, or even a suspect, we can have you picked up and taken into custody with a whole fleet of patrol cars, all with flashing lights and wailing sirens. If you were not involved in the murder, but you have relevant information, it is always in your interest to cooperate with us."

Her voice was almost a whisper. "What murder?"

"Were you lovers in June 2014?"

She didn't answer. I stood and took a card from my wallet and handed it to her. "Call me or Detective Dehan at these numbers, anytime, day or night. If we're not at the precinct, they'll forward the call."

Dehan pulled the door open. She paused as I went through it and turned back toward Dr. Wagner. "The victims were children, Doctor. Think about it."

We made our way down the marble stairs among cold echoes and crossed the gloomy hall, out into the bright, crisp noonday sun. In the car, we cut through White Plains and took Bloomingdale Road south until it became Mamaroneck Avenue. We followed that till we came to Lombardo's on the left. There I did a U-turn and pulled into the large parking lot.

"Pizza and lamb chops," I said to Dehan, "and cold beer."

She shook her head. "No, oysters, pizza, lamb chops, and cold beer."

"You're right." I nodded, and we climbed out of the ancient growler.

We found a booth and gave our order. Dehan drummed her fingers on the table and drew breath. I said, "It's too soon to start formulating theories, Dehan."

"I say to you what Nero Wolfe would say to you."

"And what would that be?"

"Phooey!"

I laughed. "Fine, let's hear it. And then you can tell me what it's based on."

The beers arrived, and she took a pull, then wiped the foam from her mouth with the back of her hand.

"You told Wagner she had pretty much confessed to having an affair with Mitchell when she refused to answer . . ."

"That was a bluff, Dehan, and has no probative value at all . . ."

"Shut up and listen, Stone. Sure, it has no probative value in court, but we're not in court. It's just you and me, nosing around. We both know if she hadn't been having an affair, she would have told us so right away." She made a scandalized face. "What, *me*? And *Brad*? Are you out of your *minds*?"

I smiled. "Fine. I'll shut up."

"Well, the same applies to the date. When we asked her if they were involved in June 2014, if they hadn't been she would have taken that way out and told us no way."

"Why?"

"Because clearly the date tied their affair to the murder in some way, might even make one of them a suspect. If the date had been wrong, she would have seized on that with both hands. Instead, she freaked out. She clammed up and told us to leave. That means one thing and one thing only, Stone. She was with him at that time."

"Maybe."

"Phooey, sir!"

"I think I preferred it when you read Mickey Spillane."

"They had an affair, and they were involved in June 2014, when those kids were killed. That's what we came here to find out, and that's what we found out. Now I am going to ask you the kind of question you ask: What was it about their being involved at that time that made us want to know?"

"I think I might have phrased it more tersely, with more brevity."

"Whatever. So what was it about their having an affair at that time that was important to us? Answer: if they were having an affair at that time, it increased the possibility that Brad might have reacted to Leroy's blackmail by killing him. Am I wrong?"

"No."

"So?"

"So we continue with the investigation, for now, but I am still finding it very hard to believe that Mitchell would kill his own daughter. Maybe when we meet him I'll change my mind. But right now it does not fit his profile at all. A liberal academic who adopts an orphan because he reads about him in the papers and feels compassion for him is not the obvious choice for killing his five-year-old daughter to cover up the murder of that same adopted orphan." She grunted, and I went on. "Besides, Sunday midmorning, with all the family there, is not the ideal time. Surely he could have chosen a better opportunity."

She grunted again. A moment later the waitress arrived with the oysters. She left, and we sat in relative silence, making only those noises you make when you're eating oysters. When Dehan had devoured the last of those edible, bivalve mollusks, and I had drawn off two-thirds of my beer, I smacked my lips and said, "There is something else."

She picked up a paper napkin and wiped her mouth. "What?"

"Lea, Mitchell's daughter, was killed with a knife."

"Uh-huh."

"So was Leroy."

"Okay . . ."

"And so were Leroy's mother and father."

She frowned hard at me. "You are reaching, Stone."

I screwed up my napkin and dropped it by my plate. "In 2019, six thousand, three hundred and sixty-eight people were murdered in the United States using handguns. Only one thousand, four hundred and seventy-six were murdered using knives.

That one small boy should be involved in four murders, each one a stabbing, is a statistical aberration, and therefore significant. It means something."

"It's a fluke, Stone. The first was a domestic incident, and the choice of a kitchen knife was opportunistic. It was what was available. And in the murder of Lea and Leroy . . ." She shrugged and watched the waitress take away the empty plates and deliver the pizza and a dish of lamb chops. When she'd gone, Dehan said, "Either the murders were committed by Mitchell or they weren't. If he did, we have to assume that he was under an intolerable amount of pressure caused by the threat of blackmail from Leroy that was going to bring down not only his family, but also his career and the clinic he was planning to establish. Now, think about it, Stone. What are the chances of a New York liberal academic having a gun in his house—or anywhere else for that matter?"

"Granted."

"You want to hear what my gut is saying?"

"Aside from 'feed me more pizza'?"

She stuffed a slice in her mouth and spoke around it.

"I think the killing of Leroy and Lea was also opportunistic. We don't know what went down that day. We only know what the Mitchells told the investigating detectives. But my gut tells me that *if* Mitchell killed those kids, it was a spur-of-the-moment decision in which he seized an opportunity and struck."

I shrugged. "It's very possible. But it's only speculation."

She stared at me a moment, chewing, then said, "Wagner will have telephoned Mitchell by now, and he'll be expecting us. We need to go see him while he is still rattled, before he has time to agree on a story with her."

I picked up a lamb chop and nodded. "That kind of thing takes a lot of time and thought and discussion. There is always something you overlook or forget about. We'll go see him after lunch."

She wiped her fingers on her jeans and reached for her cell.

"I'll call him now and tell him we're on our way, rattle him a little more."

She held the cell to her ear for a moment, sucking her teeth and staring at me. Then:

"Yeah, this is Detective Carmen Dehan of the NYPD, I need to talk to Dr. Brad Mitchell." She waited a moment, watching me. "Putting me through to his secretary." I nodded once, upward. She averted her eyes and started talking. "Yeah, good afternoon. This is Detective Carmen Dehan of the NYPD. I need to speak with Dr. Brad Mitchell . . . Oh, he's teaching a seminar right now? How long will he be?" She grinned at me and winked. "You figure he'll be another hour? So he's been in there for an hour already . . . Okay, well that's fine. Please let him know that we'll be there in an hour"—she looked at her watch—"at one thirty, and we really need to talk to him. It's important."

She hung up. We finished the chops and the pizza, drained our beers, and left.

An hour later I found a parking space outside the Psychology Building of New York University at Number Six, Washington Place. It was right next to the Center for Neural Science at Number Four. The two departments were in the same classic Gotham City style, with black facades at street level that somehow managed to suggest the deep unconscious, between massive, ochre columns in a neo-Greco-Roman style that added to the awe factor.

We found Mitchell's office on the ninth floor. He had the corner overlooking Washington Place and Mercer Street. It was large and classical in style, with a lot of mahogany and tall oak bookcases with well-thumbed hardbacks and paperbacks overflowing the shelves. The floor was dark green wall-to-wall carpet, and his desk and chair were oak and green leather.

Mitchell was tall and rangy, slim, with thick silver hair. He was standing beside his desk, in a dark blue suit, looking at us fixedly with his cell to his ear. He said, "Okay, they're here. I'll get back to you."

He hung up, laid his cell on the desk, and spoke as he removed his jacket and hung it on the back of his chair, like he was preparing for a fight.

"So, this is the new, human face of the New York Police Department. First you mount an incompetent investigation into my children's death, then you neglect it for six years, and finally, lacking any other suspects, you try to pin it on the father. That's good, you know?" He pulled out the chair and lowered himself into it. "Because I haven't been through enough in the last six years. I need to suffer a bit more." He paused, scowled at us, and asked, "What the hell do you want?"

I approached and showed him my badge. "Detective John Stone, of the New York Police Department. This is my partner, Detective Dehan. Dr. Mitchell, do you mind if we sit down for ten minutes? We'll make this as brief as is possible."

He sighed and gestured at the two chairs across his desk. We sat, and Dehan spoke first.

"Was that Dr. Wagner on the phone, Dr. Mitchell?"

He focused his scowl on her. "You know damn well it was. That's why you went to see her first, in the hopes of scaring me and unsettling me."

He loosened his tie.

I said, "Dr. Mitchell, I head up a cold-case unit at the Forty-Third Precinct. The first investigation ground to a halt through a total lack of evidence. But we have received new evidence, and we are bound to look into it."

His face flushed, and there was real anger in his eyes. "New evidence? Just what exactly do you call evidence in the New York Police Department? Rumors? Malicious gossip?"

I offered him a rueful smile. "Anything we can get our hands on, sir. It's possible we are clutching at straws, Dr. Mitchell. But in investigating the murder of two children, I would rather clutch at straws than ignore a possible lead so as not to offend somebody."

He closed his eyes and took a deep breath. After a moment he opened them again.

"I am not having an affair with Dr. Wagner, and I have never had an affair with Dr. Wagner. Does that answer your question? And please, before you go *blundering* about in your so-called investigation, bear in mind the enormous damage you could do to my career, Dr. Wagner's career, and my family. I *think*, Detectives, that we have been through enough in recent years, without this ham-fisted attempt to pin my daughter's murder on me."

Dehan raised an eyebrow. "What about Leroy?"

He frowned at her for a moment like he didn't understand what she was saying. "You mean Lee. You can't be so naïve as to think that Lee's death devastated me as much as my daughter's. I have been a psychiatrist for thirty years, and I have been in analysis for every one of those years. I am not going to sit here and lie about the most central, important things in my life. I was learning to love Lee. I certainly cared about him and his welfare. But we all knew, from the very start, that it was not going to be easy. He was a troubled and conflicted boy, and in the last year he was with us he made it *hard* to like him. Even so, Emma and I stayed the course and supported each other, and we were learning to love him."

He shook his head, and tears welled in his eyes. "But Lea . . . Not a day goes by that my heart does not break when I remember her. I long for her and weep for her. I didn't need to learn to love her. I loved her from before she was born. It's neurology, hormones, brain chemistry, whatever you like. That's how human beings work. It doesn't change the fact that she was my baby girl, I love her still, and I will love her to the day I die."

It looked sincere, but after thirty years studying the human mind and how emotions work, I was prepared to hedge my bets.

"Were you aware, Dr. Mitchell, that Lee had told his aunt, Sonia, that he believed you were having an affair with Dr. Wagner, that he had followed you to the university and taken photographs of you?"

"Yes." He gave a single nod. "I was aware of that."

"Were you aware that it was his intention to blackmail you with that information?"

"He told me that, yes. He came to my den in the house, knocked on my door, and came in. He showed me the photographs he had and told me he wanted a hundred bucks a week to keep silent about it. Otherwise he would tell my wife."

The room was very quiet for a moment. Then Dehan asked, "Do you not agree, Dr. Mitchell, that what he did provided you with a very powerful motive for murder?"

His face was like granite. He held her eye for a long moment, then said, "Yes, I do. I'd say it provides a very powerful motive for murder indeed."

Scan the QR code below to purchase KNIFE EDGE
Or go to: righthouse.com/knife-edge

Made in United States
North Haven, CT
19 November 2024

60579118R00129